One More Foxtrot

A Tale of Second Chances

Joyce Hicks

ISBN: 0692935193
ISBN 13: 9780692935194
Library of Congress Control Number: 2017914350
Encore Books, Valparaiso, IN

My profound thanks to my family Centenarians:
My father who showed me how to work hard at writing and
his sister Betty, who has been asking for a second book.

1

Daddy's Girl

Sharon D'Angelo watched women leave the Nulook salon after their weekly wash and curl, but her mother wouldn't be one of them. It had been nearly a year since Betty Miles deserted the family in Elkhart, and Sharon missed her. In a seat by the window of Sharon's Desserts, her new business, she was taking her first break since five in the morning. The cherry chip and dark chocolate cupcakes waited unfrosted as she watched her mother's crowd parade their freshened hair. *All dolled up with nowhere to go,* Sharon thought.

She enjoyed studying the street where she had spent so much time recently. The buildings were mostly three-story brick, many with the upper floors in disuse. The name of the earliest merchant was set in the cornice of the grander structures. Where fire had eliminated buildings, the replacements were one-story for new services and professional offices. Other citizens like her had felt optimistic enough to invest downtown after the local bounce back of the recreational vehicle industries. At her shop and at home whistles from frequent freight and daily Amtrak trains penetrated her windows, an omen that Elkhart's position in the Heartland on the busiest east-west route was good for business.

After her second cup of coffee, Sharon evaluated her own kingdom. *What would Daddy think?* She pondered for the umpteenth time whether she was making good on her father's investment. She backed into a corner to see the whole place at once—the counters, work area, display case, and four little tables and café chairs. The entire operation was just six hundred square feet, former home of Pie-in-the-Sky Pizza.

Her toe caught one of the chairs and it tumbled over, taking a neighbor into a clanging embrace. *Maybe a classic building would have been a smarter buy.* Sharon toyed with the thought again. She stared at the buildings across the street, fingering a corner of her apron. Vince had hoped to rehab the upper floors for apartments and give her the street level featuring a tin ceiling, bare brick interior, and creaking oak floor. *Did I owe him that?*

Twisting her gold wedding band now, she wondered if her mother, whose marriage lasted nearly sixty years, had ever felt this kind of conflict. She doubted it. Her parents' desires had meshed like well-oiled gears. In fact, her mother wouldn't have dreamed of causing it to be any other way. Untangling the chairs, Sharon reaffirmed the rightness of her location choice. It would take more than a dozen customers at a time to cut the echo in a cavernous shop. Her husband's dream of a classic remodel would have to wait.

Sharon set the chair upright with a bang. This was her time to have it her way. Her mid-fifties were in sight, a time when other women coming into their own broke glass ceilings, not tin ones, ran for high offices, and stepped up as CEOs. With childbearing years passed, the mortgage dwindling, and parents backing off—by aging gracefully or dying with dignity—clearly it was a woman's time.

"My time," she informed the cupcakes, further assured by the eggy, sugary scent of baked goods. "Isn't my fifty-three the new thirty-five, or whatever?" she went on in conversation with her image in the mirror over the counter.

Vince called her his arm candy, though she put in little time on her appearance, except for a trim and color of her curly hair at the NuLook. He said she was just naturally curvy and pretty. Privately she felt she had never come into what she might call her own style. Perhaps that could be still ahead.

Sharon hung her floury apron next to several others from her mother's collection, some dating back more than sixty years. She counted on their posy-printed faded yokes and pockets as proof of her heritage in baking. Above the hooks were decorative shelves where stood a photo of her late father, Charles Miles, and his favorite mug with Elks insignia. His knack for saving, she knew, had made this all possible for her, his princess.

Back at the front window, Sharon watched activity at D'Angelo and Sons Construction down the street where Vince's panel van pulled away. He tooted twice as he passed by her. Then his younger brother, Mike, appeared outside the construction office with their mother behind gesturing with an object. *So typical.* Sharon shook her head. *The woman would correct her sons even on the street.* For Mary D'Angelo, the boys would never be too old for a reprimand,

and Mike was very often unreliable. *Serves her right!* Sharon thought, not forgiving Mary for following her husband's deathbed wish by naming Mike as controlling son. Sharon quelled this irritation that had no recourse. Yes, Mike had three boys. She and Vince had no kids. "It's D'Angelo and Sons," Manny had said so many times from his sickbed with his relatives gathered round. Of course, the family laid Vince's lack of an heir on her, albeit gently, a point Sharon refrained from correcting in deference to their old world attitudes about manhood.

The shop phone jangled, stopping her focus on the sidewalk drama. Sharon let it ring twice. "Sharon's Desserts. How may I help you?"

"Let me speak to the person in charge."

"This is Sharon."

"I want the person I spoke to yesterday."

"I'm sure I can help you. Have you placed an order?"

"Not an order, a whole dessert buffet for an engagement party tonight. I just want to check up on the timing and delivery."

"Of course. The Lauerbach party?"

"Yes. Now, as I arranged yesterday with somebody else, I'd like the setup at noon today and the buffet promptly at seven."

"Generally, we do the setup right before the event."

"Yesterday, I specifically told the woman the setup needs to be at noon and she agreed. Maybe her English wasn't good enough to write it down."

Sharon thumbed an antacid from a tube in a drawer, crunching it up quietly. Yesterday she had asked Vince's mother to mind the shop for an hour while she made a delivery. Though Mary spoke with a slight accent, she understood English perfectly. If she agreed to new arrangements, she did it on purpose.

"I'm sorry about the confusion. I'll see what we can do."

"No, that's not good enough. I need the setup early so I can put out favors, flowers, and so forth. And I don't want dessert setup going on during the dinner. Obviously."

"I understand." What Sharon understood most of all was that without the Lauerbach party her shop was in the red that month.

"Good. Oh, yes, I expect Vincenzo to be part of the wait-staff you're providing and make the earlier delivery too."

Waitstaff? Sharon slid another antacid onto the counter. She herself provided the plating or last-minute touches and later the takedown. "Vincenzo?"

"Yes, the woman yesterday, if I understood her correctly, said Vincenzo would deliver and assist later with the Bananas Foster. Of course, he will wear a chef's apron and hat?"

For heaven's sake, the woman meant Vince. Why would his mother volunteer him for catering? The big Lauerbach house with its yawning front entry was the answer. Sharon knew the petite but imperial Lila now on the line intended her party would quash rumors about Lauerbach marital troubles at least until their daughter married. No doubt, Mary expected Vince to snoop around to see what construction jobs might be offered for the purpose of selling the house.

"I expect to light the Bananas Foster myself, Ms. Lauerbach. It's one of my specialty items."

"Oh? That's not what I understood. I hope I'm not disappointed with other aspects of the service." An extended sigh followed. "I wondered if I should have gone with a caterer with more experience."

Before Sharon could reassure her, the line went dead. What would Vince—*Vincenzo*—say about his noon hour and evening appointments at the Lauerbachs'? A change in the schedule would never have happened if her mother could have been here to answer the phone. Not that she wanted her mother full-time at her bakery as her mother-in-law was now at D'Angelo and Sons, just sometimes when she had a demonstration party or tasting. Her mother was pleasant and compliant compared to Mary, and it would have given her an outing from Shady Grove Senior Living where she was settled in—*Well, used to be.* Sharon still obsessed over the debacle of her mother's escape on Amtrak to Chicago. *Of course I can't count on my own mother for help,* Sharon fumed picturing Betty who called occasionally, made short visits, and otherwise gadded around Chicago with a Gold Coast widow or divorcée. She wasn't sure which.

Sharon set aside her irritation when the phone rang again. "Sharon's Desserts. How may we help you?"

"Hello?" Sharon said again because no one responded.

Continued silence, but not the kind from a robocall. She may have heard a breath and the words "This is—"

"Hello, may I help you?" Sharon tried again, not to risk discouraging a customer.

After a few more seconds of no response, she disconnected. This was the second, no third, call like this. None on her cell, two at home, and now, one here. She shivered, glancing at the shop's open street door.

2

A Man in Leather

*I*n a Chicago café Betty Miles sat with her hands wrapped around a latte, waiting for her friend Eleanor Goldman. She admired the lions at the entrance of the Art Institute across the street gazing benevolently on the pedestrians. Still a newcomer to city life, Betty marveled at this colorful parade and singled out individuals for speculation about their histories and secrets. Could the fortyish matron at last be pregnant? Has the man in a business suit just made a million, or been fired? Could the elderly couple be newly married?

Betty wondered if the café patrons tapping their phones made guesses about her. How little she resembled the woman who last spring had never drunk a latte or sent a text message. She thought of the shiny, loose-fitting navy suit she had chosen for her arrival at Union Station eleven months ago as a fugitive from senior fun. In Elkhart her cardigan with the cardinals had seemed like suitable attire for an octogenarian. That sweater, along with her belongings and furniture, was back in Indiana where she had broken her lease on her apartment at Shady Grove Senior Living. Though the administration had balked, her demand for a refund got their agreement. She figured it was because they bet that she would be back despite her shocking, unauthorized departure. "Begging for their forgiveness, I'm sure!" Betty muttered, recalling the consternation her decision had caused the front office and her daughter, Sharon. Today, she hoped her slim dark pants, fuchsia sweater set, and lemon print scarf fit in with other urban matrons who were out, perhaps shopping or on excursions to the symphony. She glanced toward the counter mirror. Yes, her softly curled bob—a new hairstyle for spring—was in order.

"There comes your friend now," said the barista who knew the regulars.

No one could miss Eleanor on the sidewalk. Pumpkin-colored leggings made her teal poncho even brighter, a complement to the turquoise cloche hat. Passersby stepped aside for this colorful bird of a woman leaning only slightly on her cane. Betty knew they made an unlikely pair: Eleanor's gelled hair was a bright red next to her own champagne curls; Betty's manner suggested diffidence, Eleanor's confidence.

"The usual," Eleanor called to the barista as another customer jumped up to keep the door from slamming on her. She joined Betty at her table by the window.

"How was it?" Betty grasped Eleanor's hand to hear about the doctor visit.

"He said, 'Sara, you look good to go.'"

"Meaning . . . ," Betty added her other hand to their handclasp.

"Oh, sorry! You could take that two ways. It was good news. The treatment was very successful."

"Thank goodness. How wonderful Sara can skip more ordeals. I'm happy for you, too." The sisterhood of mothering brought the women close and they hugged over the table. Betty was glad her friend was out from under the cloud of doubt about daughter Sara's health. "I know you have been very troubled by her condition."

"Not to have felt pain is not to have been human." Eleanor gestured air quotes as she offered a Hebrew aphorism that she used to cover events ranging from dire to the loss of an earring. "But you're right, I'm happy all around. It's wonderful to have a weight off my heart. I feel human enough now for ten women!"

The friends watched as a Harley coasted to the curb. Its driver removed his helmet and then rummaged in a carrier on the back. His trim black pants, jacket, and silver hair caught their attention more than did the shiny bike.

"A stud muffin," declared Eleanor.

"Not a trifle old for that category?"

"A man in leather is never too old. Now what's he doing?"

As they watched, he pulled out a teddy bear and balanced it on the handle bar. Then he backed up and took several photos of the bike parked with the busy street as landscape.

The women laughed and Eleanor knocked on the glass and waved.

He gave them a thumbs-up while they speculated on his motives.

Betty offered a travel story. "Someone once stole a concrete frog off my neighbor's porch and took photos of it all the way to New York City."

"Really! Life in a condo here doesn't have so much drama as yours in Indiana."

"The frog even went to *Cats,*" Betty went on. "The neighbor never figured out who did it. Then when the frog reappeared, she accused everyone on my street of endangering her yard ornament."

"You'd think she'd have been happy at least her frog got to a Broadway show." Eleanor hooted, which made Betty slop her coffee.

Their attention to the motorcyclist had been so zealous that he waved again, packed up his teddy bear, and rode off, the Harley growl penetrating the window.

When the women left to go to the Cultural Center for Scrabble games, they speculated further about the bear and the background for the photos. They stood a few minutes on Adams looking south. There in the parade of signs along the curb was the answer.

"Look, it says, 'Route 66 begins here,'" Eleanor exclaimed. "What I wouldn't give to be on the back of that bike hanging on. Mhmm."

Betty laughed. Eleanor never let an attractive man over fifty pass by without expressing longing. Apparently, her friend's three stints at marriage hadn't been enough.

"Actually, Route 66 didn't begin here, but on Jackson Street," Betty said.

"What? Why's the sign here then?"

"Jackson is one-way now. My Charlie always said we would take Route 66 from start to finish."

"And?" Eleanor waited to hear what excuse Betty would offer this time for her departed husband's failings.

"'Accidents never take a vacation,' Charlie always said. He was afraid a long trip away from home would be bad for his business. Insurance, you know. Reliable family man."

"But you found out that he—"

"I know. I know." Betty shrugged her shoulders. "Let's just leave it, Eleanor, okay?"

Eleanor looped her hand through Betty's arm. The friends regarded the historic sign seconds longer while waiting for the walk signal, or, as Betty called it, the sprint signal.

"Get your kicks on Route 66," Betty sang as they hiked along. How nice it would be to have a rambling route to follow now through old age, one with the kind of attractions a person would want to see—not just emergency rooms, medical appointments, and funerals.

And maybe a good man as a companion. Now that would make it perfect, she thought.

3

Beauty Shop Revelations

At eleven thirty Sharon was packing the first of the tiered servers into her car for the Lauerbach engagement party. The serving cutlery and other supplies rested in white shopping bags printed with an arty graphic of cakes and *Sharon's Desserts* in script. Vince used his key to come in the back door. *Vincenzo,* she thought.

"I can't believe you're taking time off to deliver this stuff in the middle of the day." She realized she sounded accusatory when he was doing her a favor. She changed her tactic and offered him a petit four and coffee. His mustache tickled as he pecked her cheek.

"I thought that was the arrangement. Mom said noon." Vince gobbled a second tiny cake, this one green with a pink rose.

"It certainly wasn't the original plan I had with that self-important Barbie doll, Lila. And she said you would light the bananas in a chef's hat, no less. *Vincenzo!*" Sharon crossed her arms and stared at her husband. "Does your mother call you that at work?"

"Sometimes." He raised his hands palms up, dismissive. "I'll pour on the liquor and light it. What could be easier?"

"Lots of things." The liquor ill-poured, flames ripping along the dish, then the tablecloth instead of the bananas. Or bananas turned to burnt mush. "I'll be there in the kitchen as backup."

"Don't worry, honey. I'll be the sexy paesano good with his hands that Lila, she's a-hoping for." He kissed his fingers at his wife. His lascivious grin told her that he assumed success with the Bananas Foster would lead to success in the bedroom later at home.

"Then you'd better wax the ends of your stash and put on cologne." Sharon made a quick appraisal. Though his curly hair was gone, he had kept his liquid bedroom eyes and had only the hint of a gut at fifty-three. "Just love handles, baby," he liked to say. Yes, he was still an attractive man when she had the time to look at him. *In fact, when was the last time?* But there was no time to think of that now.

His being appointed delivery boy wasn't his fault, though he could put his foot down to his mother ordering him around. But he wouldn't. Neither of the D'Angelo sons did that. Vince loaded the rest of the supplies in the car and slapped the magnetic sign for Sharon's Desserts on the door.

"I'll be home by five for a shower and change, Sharon. Hope I can get some tiling done with Mike by then. Otherwise, I'll go back tonight later."

"When are you going to tell your mother not to sign you up for delivery boy duty when you're so busy with your regular work?"

"This'll give me time at Lauerbach's to talk about kitchen upgrades."

Sharon knew she was on a tear, whether brought on by Mary D'Angelo, the lack of new catering orders, or the unnerving, breathy hang-up calls that she had kept to herself. "When your mother says, 'Jump,' you or Mike will always ask, 'How high?'" Her lips in a hard line, she glared at him.

"Give it a rest, Sharon. Mom was doing you a favor coming in to help out."

The air rushed out of her sails. Yes, this was the truth. Since her own mother was off who-knows-where, it was Mary D'Angelo who was available. Vince put down his coffee, squeezed her shoulders, and yelled "Ciao" as he left. Sharon rolled her eyes at his newfound Italian. *What next?*

With two hours to spare once the last cherry chip cupcake was frosted, Sharon set the "Back Later" sign in the window and walked across the street to the NuLook salon to see about a manicure, a luxury she still allowed herself in the killing schedule of her first year as a businesswoman. Being trapped at a nail station was enforced relaxation, if just briefly.

"So what do you hear from your mother?" Dolly, who owned the salon, escorted Sharon to a chair.

"She's having the time of her life," Sharon answered to close the subject, though she couldn't imagine what Betty was doing day to day in Chicago.

"Tell her not to do anything I wouldn't do!" Dolly elbowed Sharon lightly.

This could leave her mother quite a bit of leeway Sharon thought, looking at Dolly, who was once a sister-in-law of Vince's, one of Mike's exs. Still dressing forever twenty-nine,

Dolly was no spring chicken, but the veneer of girlishness with which she ran her shop remarkably spelled success.

Several magazines were piled on the armrest of Sharon's salon chair. Waiting her turn would be a good chance to flip through recipes in some old copies of *Midwest Living*, but noting that the chair next to her was empty meaning she could read with privacy, Sharon picked up an expensive glossy magazine whose cover promised "Five moves for the best sex of your (or his) life." Yes, spicing things up in the bedroom would be nice, though she had given little thought to whether their recent sex was the best of her life. And no doubt Vince would say the same about his side of the story. They were just too damn tired—or maybe tired of each other? Perhaps here would be some tips. A woman past fifty could use something new. She found the article that featured an unclad couple just as women took the salon chairs on either side. Sharon folded back the cover and tipped back to shield the page from view.

Tip one: "Talk sexy with your partner outside the bedroom." A few examples followed, not the sort of thing she would say ordinarily over breakfast but maybe something to try. It would be a surprise for Vince, to say the least.

Tip two: "Forget what your mother told you about—" Considering her mother told her nearly nothing, this would be easy. Sharon skimmed the page through the nonsanctioned advice. Some of the moves were, well—did anyone she knew do this sort of thing? *In Elkhart?* She glanced around the salon, her gaze falling on Dolly and a young woman with a lip cuff getting her hair nearly shaved off on one side. *Maybe they did.* She hurriedly laid the magazine facedown when a manicurist came to work on her nails. It might be bad for her dessert business to be seen reading such stuff after all.

"Irene is doing online dating now?"

Sharon glanced at the woman speaking and recognized her as one of her mother's bridge partners, Ardyce Mackleroy, who was gossiping about another woman in their crowd.

"Yes, and I hear guys expect sex even on the first date," answered the patron with her feet in lotion on Sharon's other side.

Her name, what was her name? Sharon pretended to be following a television show on the opposite wall. *Bernice.* Fortunately the sound was off so she could hear the confidences shared.

"She says some do," Ardyce confirmed.

"So?" Bernice leaned across Sharon for details.

"So, nothing. Irene doesn't kiss and tell. Smiles a lot though," Ardyce said and they both laughed.

There seemed to be sex everywhere, Sharon thought, except her bedroom lately.

"Dinner at four thirty from the senior menu and the little blue pill for dessert. Heck, the Friday fish at the VFW probably includes the little blue pill," Bernice added.

Sharon snickered as the exchange went on, thinking of a chocolate cupcake with the pill balanced enticingly in the center of green leaves. It might be the signature item for Sharon's Desserts she'd been looking for.

"Who needs the dinner? I tell you, if the guy looked right—"

Sharon took a shifty-eyed glance again. Yes, they were women from her mother's bridge group: Ardyce with her

blue waves and Bernice wearing a grandmother brace-
let with many charms dangling. She couldn't imagine her
mother engaging in this conversation. Betty looked startled
if a man wanted to shake hands.

Her nails a pearly lavender, Sharon closed her eyes as
she sat with her fingers under the hand dryer, skeptical as
always of the long-term consequences of the mysterious blue
light. Maybe it didn't matter, since her years were already
potentially shortened by stress over her business and her
mother now that Dolly, let alone these bridge women, had
reminded her of the potential for senior disasters in the dating arena. Sharon tried for a catnap with her hands impris-
oned, but a conversation between two younger women she
slightly knew kept her awake.

"How's your mother getting along these days?"

"Don't get me started. I might bite these new nails!"

"What happened?"

"Okay, I take her out for lunch every Tuesday. Afterwards
I say, 'Is there any shopping you'd like to do? Are you okay?
Do you need anything?' She always says that everything is
fine."

"So?"

"The visiting nurse calls me all officious asking if I'm
aware of mother's back pain in the morning."

"Your mom didn't tell you?"

"No. Then the nurse asks could we *manage* to buy her a
new mattress, or should she apply for township assistance?
I'm sure they think I don't look out for Mother."

Sharon's dryer stuttered as she snatched her hands out.
Her nails were not bone-dry but good enough for her to get
away from this conversational snake pit. *Do I look out for my*

mother well enough? The question popped up despite her efforts to escape. Every third Tuesday had been their lunch day together. And she thought her mother had been happy with that until she took off for Chicago on Amtrak.

"Oh, Sharon, I didn't see you here before." The speaker with the recalcitrant mother stopped her. "Didn't I hear that your mother is at Shady Grove?"

"Yes, she was. But not now." Sharon gathered her purse to discourage a familiar interrogation: Where is she living now? Why doesn't she move in with you? Aren't you worried about her? Is she all right in her mind?

Well, was she? Sharon had no idea.

Dolly stopped her on her way out. "You come back soon, Sharon. I'd love to give you a new cut and color. Your highlights are so last year." She reached up to finger Sharon's hair appraisingly. "Can't have you looking dated with your new business. Love the cute sign." She began to tap-tap in her boots to the register and turned back. "Oh, and tell Vince that whenever he's got time, I've got time."

"Pardon?"

"The sinks. They have to be ripped out evenings. Too much dust during the day. He said doing it at night would be fine with him."

"Yes, no doubt." Sharon spoke coldly then backpedaled. "I will let him know you're, uh, ready."

4

Four-Letter Words

*I*n the midafternoon, Betty patted the bronze cow that stood near the steps of the Chicago Cultural Center on the Washington Street side. The shiny bovine head and horns polished by many hands, she seemed to be walking placidly toward the park, much luckier than her ancestors who went to the stockyards.

"Just for good letters," Betty said in anticipation of the Scrabble tournament that she and Eleanor were joining at the senior center inside.

Scrabble was not Betty's best game. She was a better bridge player, and mounting the steps of the grand building, she thought about her usual foursome at the Elkhart senior center, a nondescript place with social rooms for cards and games and space for the daily hot meal delivered from the hospital cafeteria. Despite the beige interior, bridge with her friends Bernice, Irene, and Ardyce made the center a sanctuary where she supposed she would reclaim her seat sometime. This Chicago senior center had much grander quarters on the first floor of the Cultural Center that had opened in 1897 as the city's first central public library. The Washington Street entry never failed to give Betty a thrill if she walked up the shallow marble steps to Preston Bradley Hall under the forty-foot mosaic dome. On one visit, she took out her notebook to copy a passage embedded in the glass and mother-of-pearl mosaics. She wrote carefully, "He that loveth a book will never want a faithful friend, a wholesome counselor, a cheerful companion and effective comforter—Isaac Barrow." *How true!* She had underlined her observation. Her copies of *A Girl of the Limberlost* and *Jane Eyre* had been thumbed to velvet during her girlhood, but so many of the classical figures referred to on these glittering walls were still unread. Oh, she had so much to do in her time left.

Making her way along a corridor and into a spacious reading room, Betty thought about how intimidated she had felt here at first. Everyone else was busy, bent over laptops, in discussion with others, or reading books or phones. To hide how conspicuous she felt that first time, and worried about catching the attention of the security guard, she had found a scratchpad in her purse to occupy her hands as she sat. On subsequent visits, she brought a book in order to fit into this anonymous group of productive people. Not that she always read, sometimes she just sat and mused about Elkhart. As happy as she was with her stays in the city, she often felt adrift on a never-ending vacation. And now that Eleanor knew her daughter would be all right, they would carry out their plan of a family cruise in the late summer. Of course, Eleanor had invited her to go along, but it was a trip she hadn't earned by tribulation as they had, and also, she didn't want to be a fifth wheel. So she needed a plan for the coming months, something more than reading the classics.

Betty sat down to wait for the Scrabble players, and over the murmur of activity, she heard a lively tune that always made her jump to find her phone. Sharon had pointed out there was no need for panic. She could use the call log to call back. Still, she plunged her hand into her bag, feeling around for the vibrating case and finally grasping it as if it were a wiggling fish.

"Hello?" The rush of success made her somewhat breathless.

"Mom!"

"Is this you, honey?" She was still surprised by getting a phone call just anywhere and spoke too loudly at first. *Just like my mother,* she thought, picturing her shouting in the horn of their farm phone. Three minutes later she would declare her relatives in Florida sounded as if they were right next door. Betty resettled the phone more naturally against her cheek, and Sharon's voice brought her back to now.

"Yes, Mom, it's me."

"Hold on. Let me get out of the noise." Betty scuttled to a quieter area near a marble staircase.

"Where *are* you, Mother?" Sharon's voice had an edge already with the delay in conversation.

"At the senior center. You know, I told you about the Scrabble tournaments and my French culture class here."

"Oh, yes. French. Well, I wanted to talk to you about—"

Betty couldn't help breaking in. "You wouldn't believe how much I'm learning. Now I have a better idea about the names of pictures at museums. For instance, *Le déjeuner des canotiers* means 'the boaters' luncheon.' It's a beautiful painting by Renoir. Have you seen it?" Pleasure in this cultural achievement meant so much more when shared with her Sharon. Maybe they could have a walk through the Impressionists at the Art Institute where she could show off her French.

She went on. "And a wine called *pinot noir* means 'a red burgundy.' Though *noir* actually means 'black,' of course. So it should be *pinot rouge*."

"I wasn't aware you were ordering wine a lot, Mom."

"Last month, I was at a dinner buffet where the server asked if I wanted pinot noir or chardonnay. I could only shrug. But now I say, 'Pinot noir, please,' or 'Pinot noir, s'il vous plaît.'"

She wanted to describe the benefit event at a posh club, what it felt like to look out at the lights, how she felt like a tiny jewel herself on the diadem of the city that night. She wanted Sharon to have a sense of her life in Chicago with her new friends.

"Oh, I see Eleanor waving. It must be time for Scrabble." But really, even for an earthquake she wouldn't break off a conversation with her Sharon.

"Hold on a sec, Mom. Let me talk. I'm wondering if you would be coming this way soon." Sharon glanced at her schedule book, trying to figure out when she needed coverage at the shop.

"Oh, really?" Betty spoke neutrally so as to not betray her eagerness to be asked. "I hadn't actually planned yet, but I could. Plan that is. How's the shop going, by the way?" She added hastily to prolong the conversation, never mind that Eleanor was heading toward the Scrabble boards.

"Very busy. Vince's mother is helping me out but I'd—"

"Mary? She's baking with you?" Betty pictured Sharon and Mary, heads together studying a D'Angelo family cookbook. Mary offering to lend her own mother's pizzelle press. Sharon saying she couldn't possibly borrow a family heirloom. Mary insisting. Sharon hugging her and—

"Not baking, just covering the shop when I'm out."

"Oh! Well! I'm sure she's enjoying helping you." More reassuring it was, Mary sweeping up or doing dishes.

"Enjoying putting her foot in is what she's enjoying."

Betty's attention fixed on the suggestion of meddling. Sharon went on. "She actually volunteered Vince to light my signature Bananas Foster at a party. It's supposed to be my business, not an extension of D'Angelo and Sons, like, Construction and Desserts!"

"I bet he could make a big show of it." Betty laughed knowing that Vince poured a bowl of cereal with a flourish if he had an audience.

"That's not the point, Mom. Look, I've got to go." Sharon appeared to be holding a conversation with someone else too so Betty hastily returned to the tantalizing but elusive topic.

"What was it you started to ask me, dear? About my plans?"

"Never mind. Nothing we need to go over now. You call me sometime, that is, when you're free."

Now, what did that mean? Betty pressed End and dropped the phone in her purse where it fell into the disorganized heap. She had abandoned the classic lady's three-compartment purse for the sake of fitting in by carrying something more updated. Though here was another example of updated being less convenient. A bag was just what it sounded like. Everything fell into the bottom and tangled, though in the city it made sense to secure your purse over your shoulder rather than dangle it from your arm, an invitation for a snatcher. Back in Elkhart, you could leave your purse in a shopping cart and it would wait there while you looked for the peanut butter three aisles away, even if you yacked ten minutes with a neighbor.

Betty sighed and made her way to the group at the tables. She hugged Carlotta, Carole, and Andrea warmly. Though she had met them only recently, in Chicago she learned that such gestures were heartfelt. Used to these embraces, she had greeted her bridge group this way back in Elkhart on a recent trip home. Two of her friends reminded her she had seen them two days before, and another said, "Are your new city friends lesbians?" Betty had backed away, thinking of the pleasure of touch that her old crowd denied themselves.

Since there were nine women, they decided to play three to a board. Betty worried that her Scrabble efforts held back other players, but with optimism, she reached into the worn bag for her first tiles. Their satiny regularity hinted how life is full of possibilities to arrange into a coherent story, until tiles are turned over revealing an indecipherable mix, like her conversation with Sharon. She shook her head to brush away such thoughts. This time she drew *a, e, u, n, f, g,* and *x,* either a good letter or a wild card, surely. Betty laughed at her mixed game metaphor.

After keeping an *x* for several turns, Betty snapped down *axe* on an open letter *d.* "It's only four letters but feels like a triumph to use *x,*" she said. "Sixteen points."

"Thank you, Betty," Carole said, as she added an *f*, earning twenty-six points. Then Betty played another four-letter word, *guys*, on her next turn, proud to use a *y* and make a plural too. Others of her words were more pedestrian so her score was lowish.

A mild argument broke out at Eleanor's word *za* on a triple-word score yielding thirty-three points. "A slang word for pizza as in 'Let's get a za,'" Eleanor said. "It's listed in the book." She waved a dog-eared paperback of crossword gems.

"Does *ta* count for 'Let's get a margarita?'" Andrea at Betty's table mimicked bottoms up.

"Did someone say margaritas? It's five o'clock somewhere!" came from the third table.

"Actually, *ta* would count because it refers to a metallic element as in tantalite." Eleanor didn't even consult the paperback.

"What are you, in Mensa?" Carole asked as she added *pia* and a blank to complete *piazza*.

"Oh, very good!" Betty clapped and continued, "A move the Queen would envy. And I read just the other day that Prince William and Kate are very competitive too in Scrabble. Though with a family now I don't suppose they have much time."

At first Betty had felt she had nothing to contribute to this city senior group whose references ran to theater, neighborhoods, or ethnic restaurants, but soon she found her own area of expertise—the Royals—provided much diversion for her new companions.

"Well, what about this match, speaking of notables," Carole offered. "Do you think the Queen challenged Obama to a round when they met? I read that he plays Scrabble."

"Sort of like who would win, Wonder Woman versus Spiderman?" Everyone laughed.

Betty saw an opening to shine, though her Scrabble score was pedestrian. "The Queen may have already challenged a president. Nixon played Scrabble."

Favorite Nixon anecdotes were trotted out—his love for ketchup on everything and rumors that he sat fireside in the White House even in Washington summers.

As the matches ended, anarchy was breaking out. Betty was still talking about other monarchs known for their Scrabble as she played her last word, the four-letter *date* that fell on a double. For Eleanor, who by then was watching Betty's game, the word triggered a memory and she whistled through her fingers.

"I nearly forgot, girls. At six o'clock," she paused for effect, rapping a drum roll on the table, "Betty and I are going speed dating at Macy's."

Now, here was more interesting news than the winning scores, particularly to Betty. Activity related to canes, purses, and sweaters subsided.

"Oh, what fun. Lucky you, Betty." Carole, Carlotta, and Andrea gathered around Betty and Eleanor.

"Didn't know you were a fast woman."

"Your dance card will be full."

"Save at least one joker for Eleanor."

The comments fluttered like pigeons as Eleanor explained that her gourmet cooking club had organized this event in the home goods department. The babble attracted other women from the senior center and cautionary tales and opinions intertwined.

"I dated a man in my building for a while. But I don't want to take care of some old fart. I already did time."

"But look at it the other way. He would look after you when you're an old fart."

"You know, it doesn't always work out that way," the speaker went on. "I know a fellow who remarried after taking care of his wife with Parkinson's and within a year his second wife developed Alzheimer's. She had to go to a memory care unit, but his kids put up such a fuss about the expense he divorced her instead." The opinions varied at this ethical morass.

"Protecting their estate—you can't blame them."

"She didn't show early symptoms?"

"Apparently her letting him do everything covered up her confusion before they got married."

"I don't know. Abandoning her doesn't seem right. In sickness and in health, you know."

"The vows should read the other way around, health first. We're at the sickness part now as a couple. I need to get home."

Betty listened, thinking of Charlie. Generally, you assume bad things like heart disease will happen to other women's husbands, just as you assume it's other women's husbands who do bad things—certainly not your own. She had had her taste of both.

"Have a good time, Betty, Eleanor. I'll stick with women for the rest of my days," Andrea called out, raising a fist.

"Me too. I've had enough of kowtowing to men."

"Power to the sisters!" The women's voices echoed in the hallway as their sensible shoes carried them out. Betty put on a good front with a half smile. This was so like Eleanor to keep her in the dark about something she might not agree with.

"I don't know, Eleanor. Why don't you speed date and I'll catch a cab?"

"You need to meet more men, Betty. There are many fish in the sea." Yes, a sore spot, this oblique reference to the first man she had encountered in the city.

"Come on, Betty, let's go. It's advertised for seventy and up."

"Well, we're certainly the *up*. But I didn't dress for socializing." Betty compared her sweater and pants set to Eleanor's sharp combination completed by strands of silver beads.

"You would have wiggled out of this if I told you ahead. Anyway, you look like a nice Christian woman."

"I hope they're in demand at this thing." Betty again appraised her friend's colorfully stylish outfit. Eleanor was Jewish and added *for nice a Christian woman* as an appraisal for good or ill when it suited her. In this case, Betty knew it was a pan.

"Here, take these." Eleanor reached in her purse for a hot pink scarf that she exchanged for Betty's pale yellow one and clipped on two gold bracelets. They made their way along the Pedway below street level, passing shops, a fitness club pool, and a couple of restaurants. When they arrived at the food area of Macy's, Eleanor tugged the pink scarf into place again and passed along a bright lipstick, Betty complaining the whole time.

5

Just the Catering People

*P*ulling into the cul-de-sac about six thirty, Sharon thought once again about how she disliked the whole subdivision, each house outdoing its neighbor for pretentiousness. Surely the developer had thrown down a pile of magazines and chosen a house from each, whether appropriate for the geography of flat north-central Indiana, or not. The Lauerbachs' was brick faced with four white columns that looked spindly for the weight of the two-story portico where a gigantic lantern hung on a long chain.

"Tara," said Sharon.

"What?" Vince coasted into the driveway. Sharon's tendency to mutter lately irritated him.

"You know, the plantation in *Gone with the Wind.* It's the antebellum look, even a lawn jockey."

His irritation bloomed further. "You've gotta be nice, Sharon. Lila is a client, no matter her taste. And by the way," he retreated a little, "there's excellent opportunity in her center island."

"Her what?"

"Kitchen's really dated, Mom said. I could sell her a hot tap, veggie sink, roll-out composting bin, the works. So don't be touchy, okay?"

Vince was right. She must put on her best smile, but it was so hard to take these people seriously as valuable human beings. Really, did they need a wine vault, a sub-zero fridge, six-burner stove with infrared broiler, or a veggie sink? But of course, she was here with her own predilection, the art of the dessert. And you could say the same thing about it. Who needs Bananas Foster, flan, and petit fours? No one. It was just like Lila's sub-zero fridge.

Vince gave Sharon a fond nudge before such thoughts made her go home and pull the bed covers over her head. No, she would make a good show of it. A businesswoman couldn't indulge in judgments of other people's aesthetics or passions. She whispered her business plan mantra: *My desserts will be on every party table in north-central Indiana within three years.* She would carry off the evening with charm and efficiency. Vince wasn't the only D'Angelo who could schmooze.

Lila and her husband were fussing over the champagne when Sharon and Vince came through the mudroom into the cavernous kitchen. Remains of prime rib, salmon, and some side dishes sat on the counter. Apparently Lila had prepared at least some of the meal herself or hidden the catering dishes. Sharon slid around the counter to the bananas, which needed last-minute prep.

"I forgot they were Mormons," Lila was saying to her husband. "They won't want champagne. Don't try to press it on them."

"Sherry's going to be a Mormon?" He stared at a photo of a pretty blonde on the screen saver of the kitchen laptop.

"No! Just these grandparents are Mormons."

"Are they from Utah? I thought Jeff's family was from Illinois."

"I explained all this to you before."

"Here, I'll get out seltzer and juice for them," her husband said, opening the fridge. Sharon moved the cutting board and fruit to the doomed center island.

"You can't offer people orange juice for a toast. Get away from the cupboards. I'll find something else. Isn't he an idiot, Vincenzo?" Lila slammed a bottle of sparkling grape juice on the counter, addressing Vince as if he were in on a joke. He raised his eyebrows slightly.

"We-e-e-ell," Lila's husband purred, "Peanut, you always have a good idea." Sharon turned aside as he tried to nuzzle Lila's ear. "You figure it out."

"Stop it! Now listen, uh, Sharon, is it? Better pour the brandy on the bananas out here."

"But—" Then remembering her resolution, Sharon said, "You just give us a signal when you're ready. Your daughter looks very lovely, by the way."

"Yes, of course she does." Lila's smile was tight.

Her husband turned to Sharon and Vince, seeming not to have noticed them before. "Lila, introduce me to these kind people."

"Sharon D'Angelo and her husband, Vincenzo. This is Del."

"So nice to meet you, Sharon." He shook her hand. "Our little girl has gotten engaged tonight."

Still holding Sharon's hand, he addressed Lila, "Peanut, get them champagne glasses. Come have dessert with us!" With the excuse to arrange the bananas, Sharon was able to pull away.

"Del, these are the catering people." Sharon could feel the scorn even at a distance.

"Well, invite them another time for dinner. Lila loves to entertain." Del beamed at his wife, shook Sharon's hand again, and ambled back though the great room door to the guests.

Clueless. Sharon caught herself before speaking aloud. Lila was still hovering around Vince. Sharon saw she held something blue behind her back.

"Vincenzo, I have a little something for you. And where is your chef's hat?"

He put it on, and Lila stood on tiptoe to tie a blue-striped bandanna around his neck. "I got this in Venice last summer. Now we're ready for the dessert, Sharon."

From her expression, Sharon could tell this was Lila's defining moment of entertaining that evening. Sharon handed the lighter to Vince and crossed her fingers. Soon the *oohs* and *aahs* told her that the fruit conflagration oozing in its perfect sauce was a success added to by heavily inflected remarks from Vince. If he could have broken into an aria, he would have.

Sharon would have been very surprised to learn that her mother was speed dating while she was dealing with the Bananas Foster.

6

A Few Good Men with Blue Cards

Twelve female speed daters sat at tables for two in the food court of the department store. Each table had a pink card and a number—Betty's was nine—and a dozen men had blue cards and a list detailing their route through the tables. Betty surveyed her competition. Several women were dressed rather theatrically: one with yellow-framed half glasses and a necklace of large turquoise and another in a leather skirt over leggings. Betty admired a little black dress and felt a stab of nostalgia upon seeing a sweater with cardinals since hers had not made the migration to Chicago.

She looked over the pickings among the men. One wore a Mr. Rogers sweater. Others were in crew neck shirts pulled tight over bellies, and another one looked as if he would be more comfortable on his yacht. A scrawny fellow had his belt nearly under his armpits. All presumably were living alone and had gotten themselves together for this occasion as best they could. There was a smattering of canes, a walker, and a wheelchair.

What am I doing here? Betty asked herself. She could offer no conversation about gourmet cooking or European travel. She wasn't even from Chicago but was a Hoosier, for heaven's sake, the dumbest state resident nickname in the country.

Ting, ting, ting! A bell rung by the gourmet club president sent the contenders out of the gate with their blue cards. Betty sat up straighter and folded her hands on the table. When one of the crew neck shirt men approached, she half stood so he could introduce himself.

"Ed Conley, pleased to meet you." He pumped her hand, then sat down, resting his stout arms on the table. "I'm supposed to tell you something about myself. Well, I enjoy fly fishing." He smiled at her.

"How interesting. My late husband fished a little." Oops, she just broke dating rule number one. Don't talk about your previous spouse.

"Is that so?" A silence threatened.

"Where do you like to fish?" Betty ventured a lure sure to hook a big one. As she guessed, this reeled in an exchange about Michigan versus Wisconsin, and both were surprised when the bell tinged again. Though he seemed pleasant, he might prefer a woman in waders over a woman taking French, Betty concluded.

Date number two was a downright handsome man with a shaved head, the kind of man in advertising portfolios for retirees.

"Emery Fielding. And you?" He held the chair for her after a neutral handshake.

"Betty Miles. Are you part of the gourmet cooking club?" She decided to speak up first, though his good looks were a little off-putting.

"Only if you count grilled peanut butter sandwiches as gourmet." He had the build of a man who works out. And his belt rode in the right spot.

"Oh, that sounds yummy."

"Yes, it has a piquant flavor of peanuts and butter."

"With hint of burnt toast and is complimented by a pinot noir." Betty touched her thumb to forefinger and burst out laughing. Maybe this evening would be fun.

"At least we can *talk the talk*," he said. "My daughters signed me up for this. 'You should be getting out more by now, Dad.' So here I am. Tell me about yourself."

So a fresh widower, Betty concluded, but one with a sense of humor.

Betty wasn't sure what Sharon would think of speed dating, or any kind of dating, for her mother. Perhaps it would seem too strange, or maybe even disrespectful, to see someone other than her daddy with her mother—like a dog walking on its hind legs, a novelty true, but wrong. Dating might be all right for other mothers but not for hers was how Sharon would feel, Betty was sure. But Sharon wasn't in sight right now, so—

"I'm from Indiana actually. I'm staying with a friend in the city."

"A Hoosier! From Da Region?" She shook her head.

"The Fighting Irish?"

"Oh no, further east than Notre Dame. Elkhart."

"The Amish!"

"Yes, I suppose the Plain People are our claim to fame." Betty despaired. Upcoming would be a conversation about the buggies and so forth. "But this year I have spent a lot of time in Chicago living with my friend." She gestured toward Eleanor.

"Ah, that is the ideal. A friend to visit here and a home in the country." They weighed city and country, concluding both had charms. He shook her hand warmly as the bell sounded to move on.

Next came High Belt. *Maybe it's keeping him upright,* Betty thought. After introductions, a lecture ensued on his former ailments that grew from an unbalanced gut. One thing led to another. Had she tried the cave man diet or a fruit flush? Mushrooms? And of course he did a detox at least once a month. So refreshing! Right now he was on minimum intake and had never felt better. Energy for bicycling, swimming, and sex. *It would be like loving up a lizard,* Betty thought and stood up to excuse him even before the bell rang.

Another man with fleshy ear lobes that made her think of a basset hound got to the point immediately. He was looking for a lady and had "a real nice" house with a new kitchen. Two big flat screen TVs with satellite—one in the master bedroom—and a washer and dryer near the master bedroom. No stair climbing to do laundry in this house. He'd have to say his late wife had an eye for decorating, so everything looked "real classy." Eating out like he did now was all right, but home cooking was best. Why, his place had a breakfast nook and dining room both. It would be "real nice" to have someone to share it with again. *Someone who wouldn't want to change a thing,* Betty thought, *including his late wife's photo on the dresser.*

The bell tinged men to and fro. Several she quite liked: one who took senior scholar tours, another enrolled in Chinese cooking and wore a Mr. Rogers sweater, and the witty closet gourmet. Perhaps some of the men liked her too. But it seemed impossible to want to cuddle up with any of them. Perhaps Sharon was right and AARP was wrong. It was too late for a second time around and quite probably unseemly too.

After the last bell, the energetic woman in charge of the evening asked everyone to sit down. Betty and Eleanor found each other.

"Not a stud muffin in the bunch!" Eleanor spoke in a stage whisper.

"What about that one?" Betty tipped her head slightly toward Emery, who had been the most intriguing to her.

"That chrome dome look. Well, it does something for me on Bruce Willis, so that one's a clear *maybe*."

"It's déjà vu all over again!" Betty sighed dramatically.

"Why?"

For Betty, they were fifteen again, sitting in a drugstore booth comparing notes on favorite boys. And she and Eleanor liked the same one! Eleanor laughed at her observation, but in truth they could feel the whole room bristling with competitive preening. As the next speed dating step, gentlemen would provide blue cards with their contact information to ladies with whom they wished further acquaintance.

Tension grew even higher as men made final surreptitious evaluations and filled out the cards and put them in envelopes. The women sat a little straighter chattering among themselves, a picture of nonchalance.

Betty slid out of her chair and, with a feigned cough, said she needed a drink of water. Out of sight, she opened her bag to paw around for her wallet. Yes, safe in the back compartment was the fiftieth anniversary photo of her and

Charlie. Betty looked critically at the old photo. She had shopped in South Bend for her outfit, which had been quite a splurge, a blue jersey dress and white jacket. Charlie had on a grey suit. She looked closely at their expressions. They were smiling, the picture of a lifetime of happiness, but now she saw it as a static photo dated in its affect as well as wardrobe—shoulder pads in her jacket raised her corsage so it nearly met her earlobe.

She sighed. The photo offered no message from the grave, such as permission to date, but simply recorded two people happy on that day at that moment, a museum piece sealed in time. But time had moved on, like the styles. She rearranged the pink scarf on her sweater so that its scoop neck showed off her fine collarbones and heart-shaped locket from Charlie. She hurriedly packed away her wallet and marched back into the group just as blue envelopes were placed on her table. Betty opened them, hopeful as a teen on Valentine's Day. The homeowner of generous earlobes provided his contacts; thankfully High Belt did not. The good-natured angler asked for her number and email. Well, if she agreed to meet him, they would not be short of conversation. There would always be another fish story. And Mr. Fielding had expressed interest in her—clearly the most sophisticated man, quite possibly the only one Eleanor considered suitable for an outing. At the end, some women handed their pink cards around to request or provide contacts, but Betty and Eleanor refrained. The blue cards and their authors needed much more scrutiny.

Eleanor got right to the point. "How's your score, Betty? I've got at least one live one. The others you can have."

"Really Eleanor? Then it's like my mother often said." Betty shook her head, her expression feigning resignation with her lips a thin line.

"What did she say?"

"'Each to her own choice said the woman—'" Betty paused.

"Well, naturally."

"'—*as she kissed her cow.*'"

"Oh, you got me on that one! You old fox!" Eleanor threw her arm around Betty. The two women then compared their top choice. Of course, it was Emery Fielding.

7

A Midnight Intruder

About twelve thirty, Sharon rinsed off the plates she and Vince had used for a late-night supper. Prime rib for Lila's guests, grilled cheese sandwiches for them. But Vince's grilled supreme sandwich was a guilty pleasure— thick slices of sharp cheddar on sourdough bread between tomato and onion slices slathered with mayo and mustard then pan grilled in plenty of butter. As she flicked off the kitchen lights, Vince called something from upstairs.

"What?"

"Would you like—"

"Wait. What?" The whistle blasts from the Amtrak train crossing their block and the next one cut off his question. A third whistle set would soon sound as the eastbound train approached the station where a few sleepy passengers would board and a few Elkhart residents would get off laden with luggage or shopping bags from their trip to Chicago. She didn't bother to wait for the quiet that would come after the final signals and headed upstairs to their bedroom. Whatever he was saying, he could ask her face-to-face.

"How about a back rub for my dessert lady? Where's your lotion?" The success of the Lauerbach event, both the desserts and a potential costly kitchen overhaul, called for further celebration.

"Sounds nice, but you're tired too." Sharon kissed him lightly.

"We'll sleep when we're dead. Roll over this way." He slid the nightgown straps off her shoulders when she got into bed. "Just a back rub."

"Sure, right, Vincie." His hands were already denying this simple intention, and she was straining to stay awake when the doorbell rang.

"What the hell?" Vince sat up.

"Maybe it's just a kid pranking us." Sharon got out of bed to look out the window. The bell sounded again after a polite interval and was followed by tentative knocking.

"There's no car out front."

"I'll go see." Vince pulled on a shirt and shorts.

"Maybe we should just call the police." Sharon reached for the phone when the knocking got more forceful.

"Hold on. Hold on," Vince shouted down the stairs. "Don't call yet, Sharon."

"Take the shotgun, Vince." She got it out of the closet and handed it to him.

"Probably some guy too drunk to see shit from shinola. Thinks this is his place," Vince said.

Likely, your brother, Mike, Sharon thought, but didn't say so.

The house was silent for a minute or two. Vince had put down the gun and started for the bed when the bell rang again.

"Be careful, honey. It might be that guy you're suing."

"I doubt it. Maybe you shorted a cupcake of frosting and they've come to get you," Vince tossed toward her and headed downstairs without the gun.

Tiptoeing across the hall, Sharon went down the top five steps toting the Remington, finding it awkward to hold in any position that could be considered covering her husband.

Apparently, Vince had gone out on the front porch. She came down the last few steps and sidestepped into the dining room, keeping her body out of sight but the barrel aimed at the door. The tone of the voices suggested negotiation. One was female, excited. Sharon got a better grip on the gun, listening for any sign Vince was in trouble.

The front door opened.

"Sharon?" Vince called toward the stairs. "You better come down here." Ahead of him, a girl stepped in the entry, facing squarely toward the weapon. Already in tears, she shrieked, backing into Vince.

"Jeeezus, Sharon, put that down. This girl's looking for you. What did you say your name is?"

"Olivia. But I go by Livy. Livy Graveswell-Riley." Her tone struck Sharon as full of false bravado.

"Do we know you?" Sharon regarded the young woman in black yoga pants and grey tunic. A streak of shocking pink ran through the right side of her dark brown hair that fell to the tips of her ears. She had dumped a backpack on the hall floor.

"No, not face-to-face because my family is so sucking high-and-mighty conservative. Their crap doesn't smell, you know?" She paused adding, "Pardon my French."

The D'Angelos were silenced by this revelation.

"What family is that?" Sharon looked at Vince who shrugged. It wouldn't be the first time some of his people, or people of his people, turned up. Now that the young person was indoors, they could see their visitor was hardly out of girlhood.

"So, you know one of my cousins, like Joe or Pete, or my brother, Mike D'Angelo?" Vince asked. She shook her head.

"Their kids?"

"I never heard of any of your family at all." She gestured toward Vince. "Only Aunt Sharon. I guess that's you, Aunt Sharon, or are you divorced from her and this is someone else?" she addressed Vince.

"Excuse me?" Sharon had propped the gun against the wall. Surely she wasn't hearing right. "Who is your family? I think there's a mix-up here. We don't know a Riley family."

"Then you've heard of the Graveswells? My grandmother is Irene Graveswell."

Sharon shook her head.

Vince took up the thread. "I'm sorry, young lady, but you'll have to give us more to go on here. Let's go in the kitchen. Maybe we can call these people for you." He urged them all in that direction.

"How did you get here so late?" Sharon asked as she poured milk in a kettle. Hot chocolate might help sort this out. She glanced at the kitchen clock. After one already and she had three dozen cinnamon rolls rising to bake by seven o'clock for the monthly pastors' breakfast at nine.

"On Amtrak from Chicago. It was my bad to forget about the time change. So sorry, Aunt Sharon." The girl didn't look tired at all to the older couple.

"Look, I don't have any brothers or sisters. So, I'm sorry, but you're not my niece," Sharon said evenly. "Would you like to call someone else?" She pointed toward the phone.

The faster this thing could be sorted out, the better. Vince was obviously relying on her to solve the mystery since he had begun to set out sandwich materials again, his usual fallback. Maybe they could drive the girl to these other people.

"Well, God, maybe I'm your niece, maybe not. That's what I'm here to find out. Like I said, Grandma and Mom are always so 'we're not going to bother them.'"

The girl got up and walked around, touching the counter top appliances, opening a cupboard or two. "You've got a way cool kitchen." She began to pull knives from the block holder, admiring each and putting it back until Sharon shoved the block out of her reach. "Then when I found out about the college money," she made a move to hug Sharon, "I wanted to meet you even more."

In the girl's travels around the kitchen, she removed a bottle of wine from a rack to squint at the label. "I'm not, you know, the most tactful individual. But I do know a person should always say 'thank you' for a gift." She set the wine down. "So thank you, Aunt Sharon—I can't thank your dad since he's dead obviously—for helping me go to my dream college."

Sharon placed the wine back in the rack. It was a good bottle of sauvignon, she noted wildly as she sought a focus for her cartwheeling brain.

"Any thoughts, Vince?"

"Here's what I see: three people dog-tired. Let's just work this out in the a.m. Honey, how about making up a bed for, for her," he gestured with a nod, "in the family room?"

While the girl was in the bathroom, a whispered argument occurred—was she, or wasn't she dangerous—a compromise resulted that had Sharon hiding the knife block in the garage, then getting out sheets and a blanket. Despite her guest's protestations that she could just sleep under her jacket on the floor, Sharon opened the sofa bed. Vince retrieved the shotgun from the dining room and waited by the stairs until Sharon was ready to go up. Completely fatigued by the peculiarity of the situation, she said little once they got upstairs.

"I'll call Mother in the morning. Maybe she's heard of these people," she mumbled then fell into a deep sleep.

Vince lay awake cataloguing the cast of characters the girl referred to. It was unlikely that she was connected to his relations—no mysterious college money coming from them. On the other hand, Charlie Miles, Sharon's father, turned out to have been quite the saver. Over the years Vince had sized him up as a wily guy, pillar of the community, yes, but with excessive reserve about his finances, which his wife and daughter saw as merely old-fashioned gallantry. A year ago, there was the surprise of the savings bonds that seeded Sharon's business venture. Perhaps Daddy Warbucks's generosity extended outside the family too, Vince considered. *But why?*

He rolled away from Sharon. Though the house had fallen into darkness, it seemed to be a restless peace, the creaking contractions or realignment of walls and roof signaling minute forces at work, as if that which was hidden was coming to the surface. Even the pesky red squirrel in the attic chewed to the rhythm of his thoughts.

Was the girl downstairs asleep, or was it her restless thoughts meeting his that kept him awake?

8

Betty Plays a Blue Card

Though Sharon was loathe to leave the stranger in her house when she went to her shop at six, one peek at the girl, who was even younger than she had thought last night, reminded her that teenagers slept heavily and late. Besides, Vince was up already and would be home until eight. They could confer about the situation on the phone. *But this mystery must be solved immediately,* she thought, sorting the reasons for no delay.

They could be harboring a runaway or even a thief. Who knew what this kid might have done? Her claims of kinship seemed wildly improbable. If her reference to college money were true, maybe a scholarship had provided a name that had nothing to do with them at all, just a coincidence in spelling.

At her shop, she baked cinnamon rolls and as usual drank coffee from the Elks mug, a tribute to their father-and-daughter Saturday breakfast excursions. On his way to warm up the car, her father always said to her mother, who was still in her bathrobe, "Tell Her Majesty that her coach is waiting by the door."

He often surprised Sharon with a different diner, sometimes driving them to a truck stop where, according to him, the "Eat" sign forecast good sausage gravy. Other times he may have spotted a little place where Amish women made scrapple served with real maple syrup. *Are these places all gone?* Sharon pondered as she slid more trays into the oven. Really, she and Vince should take country drives the way they used to.

As Sharon whipped up vanilla glaze, in Chicago Betty lay abed at the edge of consciousness. Dreams of her former lives sometimes left her unsure which bedroom, which lifetime, she was in. Until opening her eyes this morning, Betty felt the bed to be her marital one with Charlie at her side. But instead of the plain maple dresser, a mahogany armoire was across from the bed, reminding her she was at Eleanor's condo. The pretty bedroom had multi-paned windows that turned Lake Michigan into a stack of postcard views. She had stayed here so often over the last year that this guest bedroom room was now referred to as "Betty's room."

Betty often organized her day before getting up, and recently she found it more important than ever since figuring out how to fill the day was often a challenge. She had taken to jotting a list in a blue daybook.

Betty read over today's list: *Breakfast with E. Tidy up room. Take E.'s dry cleaning to concierge and pick up mail. Ask E. about library books. Leave for French class 1 p.m.—*

"And what else?" Betty said aloud.

The housekeeper did many of the little tasks that formerly felt tedious, but she now realized gave the pleasure of usefulness to many hours.

"What else?" She tapped her pencil on the nearly blank page.

Though she may not have said it aloud before, this question niggled at her greatly. What was she doing living in the lap of luxury on Lake Shore Drive? Though she liked Eleanor immensely, was her final role to be companion, as in a Victorian novel? The valued crone who kept track of the steamer trunks, adjusted the pillows on madam's wheelchair, and ordered around the servants?

What should I be doing? she wrote and underscored. The appropriate options for her seemed limited.

Without grandchildren or great-grands, she had no responsibilities in childcare, a role many of her Elkhart colleagues fulfilled in this day and age where everyone worked. Sharon, knee-deep in her new business and with Vince's mother at hand down the street, didn't really need her mother too.

Betty checked the time. Sharon was probably up early right now at her shop. It would be fun to call just to say good morning, but she resisted. No, she didn't want to be a bother at a busy time at Sharon's Desserts.

Betty took as much pride in the cute shop and growing clientele as if she were organizing each aspect herself. To anyone who would listen, she extolled her daughter's virtues as a culinary artist and businesswoman. "She's always been so creative with fancy food. Her French apple tart—well, tarte aux pommes—is a buttery dream and a work of art with the sliced fruit on top."

Sharon's business card was tucked in the frame of Betty's dressing table mirror and she reached for it. *How proud Charlie would be! If only he had lived longer.* Betty ran her fingers over the embossed card trying to keep other if onlys quiet, but they rattled around like loose marbles. This morning's scanty to-do list made corralling these thoughts impossible.

If only Charlie had given Sharon the savings bonds personally instead of stashing them in a safe-deposit box in Chicago. *And if only* he hadn't also left bonds there for that simpering and stylish banker, Irene Graveswell, his affair—or whatever it was—would have stayed hidden. Up until that moment last year in the bank's chilly vault, Charles L. Miles had been to her a perfect husband and father. These regrets always led Betty to one conclusion: Make sure Sharon never finds out about the Graveswell woman.

Betty closed the daybook with its short to-do list and looked resolutely at the blue cards from men who wished to see her again.

"Two by two," she said pondering the natural order of companionship. There were pleasures in it and, yes, pains, but perhaps this was the meaning she sought and was as well another tactic of staying out of Sharon's way. She had tried assisted living, and now she would try a boyfriend.

Betty felt energized by the decision that required two other immediate considerations—which man or men—to alert that she was available for further acquaintanceship and what to wear while doing so. A lovely handwritten note to each on her personal stationery seemed like the right touch, but an exchange could take a week. *I'm ready now,* she thought. Phoning a man seemed very modern but didn't leave wiggle room. She could be stuck stammering a refusal on the phone if he suggested a 5K walk or a wrestling tournament. Email left more ways to retreat though the mail lasted forever, as she had been warned in her computer class.

"Emailing seems best," Betty informed the blue cards, but this still didn't answer the question of which Romeo to choose. She flipped through them again. The man of the floppy earlobes looking for a companion-housekeeper, and Ed Conley, the happy angler, and the cardigan sweater guy who was learning Chinese cooking, and the handsome Emery Fielding—these men were her possibilities.

Since it was too early to email no matter which was her choice, as a note sent before eight might suggest desperation, she decided that some girl talk with Eleanor would firm up her choice. Also, she could pussyfoot around the delicacies of the blue card from Mr. Fielding, who had unknowingly set up a competition between the friends.

Hanging around in her bathrobe was not Betty's style, but what to wear, what would make her feel brave enough to actually email a man? Thinking about doing it was one thing, and actually doing it quite another. She sifted through several pairs of limp slacks. *No!* Then she considered her newest skirt and matching sweater to put her in the mood to date. This outfit seemed unreasonably optimistic—perhaps a jinx, even. Then her hand fell on her newly acquired yoga pants and silky lavender tunic. A woman in yoga pants was a woman with spirit, and at her age, nerve.

They were a little hard to get on, but she was pleased with the slimming effect and headed to the kitchen to find Eleanor.

"Well, namaste to you too!" Eleanor said, pouring their coffee. "You're ready to greet the sun or something?"

"I've decided to date."

"It's about time. Are you looking for a yogi?"

"Ha-ha! The men from speed dating, of course. But I can't decide which ones." This might give her friend a chance to say she should contact Emery.

"Let's review the contenders," Eleanor said.

Betty shuffled through her cards. Judging a man by his earlobes was wrong but not by his wife-ready home.

"His late wife's recipe for chicken à la king is probably on the counter for you now," Eleanor said. His card went to the bottom of the pile.

They debated men's merits further. Was a widowed man better than a divorced one? Did scintillating conversation compensate for chronic phlegm or modest income? And what about mobility like driving and walking a few blocks? Income, health, marital status, or sport of choice—these qualities were indiscernible from the blue cards.

"Maybe a few minutes of downward facing dog would help," Eleanor said finally.

"I guess I'll just pick fisherman Ed. He seemed good-natured. Maybe I'll send to the handsome one, Emery, too," Betty said after noticing that Eleanor expressed interest in neither suitor.

Betty's donning her yoga pants and Sharon's making glaze coincided with Vince checking the hide-a-bed where he expected to find the girl still asleep. Instead she was in the kitchen making French toast. Freshly cut oranges were in a dish on the counter.

"I always cut oranges into smiles. Way fewer calories than squeezed." She arranged them in a happy sunburst. "Did you know a glass of fresh-squeezed has, well shit, three hundred calories or more? I mean you wouldn't sit down and eat half a dozen oranges, so why scarf up that many in juice?" She looked at him expectantly.

"I guess sliced is better," he said, thinking he'd heard this lecture before about the fresh-squeezed juice that he loved.

"So how many pieces of toast, Mr. D'Angelo? People call me Livy, remember?"

"Uh, three, I guess, Livy." Sharon allowed him two, but after his restless night he needed fortification.

"I like to use a nutty bread, but wheat was all Aunt Sharon has." The girl let a pat of butter melt on each golden piece, added maple syrup, and passed the plate to Vince.

"Thanks. Now about your, your relationship to us."

"I was thinking, Mr. D'Angelo, you're probably my Uncle Vince." She dug into a stack of toast.

"It's all right to tell me if my brother was, well, if you're related to my brother. Mike had several girlfriends." Vince felt this possibility needed absolute elimination.

"No, like I said last night, my grandmother, Irene Graveswell, says she knew Mr. Miles, Sharon's dad. And in my humble opinion, she means *knew* in the Bible way." Vince's expression of understanding was tentative.

"Like in they had sex. And that resulted in *begetting*. And that's why he left money to her, and she gave the money to my mom, who gave the money to me for college tuition. And that's why I'm here to thank you guys."

To Vince, her recital sounded like the song his nephews liked about the old lady who swallowed the fly. He took time to think.

"I don't know. That's a lot of speculation that doesn't make us your aunt and uncle. Maybe Mr. Miles gave a scholarship to your college?" This seemed out of character for Charlie Miles, but people did act charitably, especially near death.

As she poured more syrup, Livy led him on a journey of overheard conversations, whispered innuendos, yearly visits in her childhood by the nice man Chuck, and leaps in logic that made Vince's head spin. If any of it were true, Charlie's sainted rep was in the dust.

"Your mom or grandma never contacted my mother-in-law or my wife?"

"Nope. They have too much class for that, they always say."

"That's a point, I guess." And fortunate too, he thought, since Betty would not be able to imagine such a charge about her husband.

Putting emphasis on the pronouns, Livy replied, "Here's my point. It's unfair to me, Mom too, to be in the dark about our genes."

Oh, genes, thought Vince. Fortune-tellers of all sorts of inevitables a person might not want to know. And what guarantee did genes give, anyhow? His family came from Sardinia, which was now known as a blue zone. He'd seen on television that people in that area lived well past one hundred. Well, his father had died at seventy-seven from cancer, genes be damned.

"Is my mom's father, Arthur Graveswell or Chuck Miles?" Livy's voice that was pitched for the balcony with this question alerted him to the dangers of this line of exploration right now. Sharon was on the brink of success or a nervous breakdown in the efforts of her business. Vince feared a major distraction might send her over the edge.

"Maybe this idea is kind of shortchanging your Grandpa Graveswell's legacy, Livy."

"That's the thing. He died before my mom was born."

"Oh?"

"Yeah. The story at our house is that my mom was a surprise baby way after her brother and sister. Grandpa Graveswell never even knew about it, which I guess you could say the same about the 'L' train that hit him."

"Uh-huh." Vince could see the potential for a train wreck here too.

"I'm not wanting genetic testing. I just thought if I met your wife, I would know for sure. Everyone says I'm psychic." Livy crossed her hands under her chin.

Vince studied her for a second-generation resemblance to Sharon but saw nothing specific. Perhaps she took after her father, whom she had not mentioned in this scenario, he noted.

"I see." He had squeezed three oranges during this disclosure, forgetting the calories. "Okay, let's let things ride as they are now. Mr. Miles gave a scholarship and you're here to thank us. Never mind bringing up the other story thing now with Aunt, uh, Sharon, uh, Mrs. D'Angelo. We'll break that to her gently."

"You think she won't like me, you mean?" Livy's pink hair fell over her face.

"I just mean she might be distressed to think her father had a lady friend in Chicago."

"Got ya, Uncle Vince. I mean Mr. D'Angelo. Can I go over to see Sharon's Desserts now?"

"Shouldn't you go home or to class? The Chicago bus leaves around noon."

"I'm on quarter break so I can stay a few days." Her smile was a light going on under her pink hair. "Isn't that cool?"

Vince agreed this news was indeed cool. As he gathered specs for his workday, she tidied the kitchen with such vigor that the French toast was only a memory.

9

Close Encounters of Some Kind

As fortification for emailing a gentleman, Betty decided on a brisk walk to the French bakery for almond croissants. A half a block toward the bakery, what she yearned for, however, was a really sloppy cinnamon roll torn from its neighbors, its edges ragged and dripping with frosting. *Indiana homey.*

As if conjured by her mother's desire over a hundred miles away, Sharon, who had drizzled topping on the last bun, pressed her phone icon for her mother. Betty heard Sharon's ringtone, "Somewhere over the Rainbow." For once, she caught the phone on the first plunge into her bag and before the last notes.

"Hello, honey. I was hoping you'd call." After a year with her phone, Betty found she could amble along the street and talk too.

"Hi, Mom. What are you doing?"

"I'm walking to La Petite Patisserie, but oh, I'd like one of your cinnamon rolls instead."

"There are three dozen right in front of me."

"Pastors' breakfast day."

"How do you remember that date? I hardly do."

"Men's groups work like clockwork. Kiwanis—third Thursday. Downtown Boosters—second Monday. Insurance associates—last Friday. Your father never missed a meeting. I suppose there are women in the groups now."

"Yes, about a third of the pastors are women, actually."

"Speaking of dates, Sharon, I wanted to tell you about last night."

Betty had worried about a conversation opener to talk about dating with Sharon. Though Eleanor said her social life was none of her daughter's business, Betty wasn't so sure. Sharon had been very close to her father. The slightest hint of someone's taking his place, even as a dinner companion could be upsetting. And it was obvious Sharon's nerves might be on edge, what with her new business on top of managing her home and Vince. But if approached the right way, maybe Sharon would be receptive. It could be such fun to chatter about the details with her daughter.

"This might be a surprise to you, dear, but last night I went speed dating and—"

"A train is going by. Hold on a sec."

Betty could hear the seductive whistle. The Lake Shore Limited, her own Yellow Brick Road last spring to a new city life, was on its way to Chicago. She hoped the dessert shop would be a similar talisman for Sharon.

"Did you say *dating*, Mother?"

"Speed dating. Maybe you haven't heard of it. You talk to each man about ten minutes and then change partners. I met about a dozen men and now I can choose—"

"Was this online? Did you give any personal information?"

"This was at Macy's."

"You met strange men at Macy's?"

The hoped-for girl talk had become an interrogation. "They weren't strange, honey, well maybe one was with his colonic purges, but the rest seemed nice."

"Did you give any personal information? Address? Phone?"

"Well, not much, not yet." Betty hoped Sharon was occupied with some task at hand that would divert her focus a little.

"Mother, for heaven's sake! You're in a big city. You can't just give your name and address—whatever it is now—to men at Macy's."

"I'm trying to tell you this was through Eleanor's gourmet cooking club. Not men off the street. Let me say one complete sentence, please."

"Sorry. Go on." Sharon sounded repentant, so Betty plunged in with more detail.

"Several men want to see me again and I'm deciding which one to try out first."

"Try out?"

"Yes. Get together. It's just lunch or dinner, honey, to see if we have anything in common. Would that bother you?" When a longish silence followed, Betty sat down at an outdoor table at the bakery.

Sharon was picturing her mother lunching. Yes. That sounded harmless, but beyond that were dangers. Did her mother know the new first-date protocol for seniors that she had heard about at the hair salon? And from Betty's bridge partners, no less.

As Sharon paced her shop while she dealt with her mother, Vince's van pulled up. She watched the Olivia girl get out while Betty was describing some man who reminded her of a basset hound. Sharon tried to appreciate her mother's vivid description.

"He had a house he wanted to show me." Betty re-created the imagined scene of his wife's recipe already set out on the counter. She waited for a giggle from her daughter. Silence again stretched out instead.

Sharon watched the girl pause at the van door to tell Vince something. He smiled and nodded. She tried to remember the name the girl had given them last night, a surname with an unpleasant association—Wells. No, Graves.

Betty chattered on, describing a man taking Chinese cooking classes who wore a sweater "just like Mr. Rodgers." Did Sharon think she should contact that one, or the handsome one, or the man who liked fishing?

Sharon made no response.

"Honey?" Maybe this discussion was a mistake altogether. Eleanor's advice may have been right.

Sharon was thinking of her own father, who found fishing dull and would have said a man taking cooking classes needed a hobby or was "funny." A man should be doing—helping with a civic event, making repairs around the house, or tinkering in his workshop while listening to a game on an old radio. Her father had liked Vince so much, and the four of them had gotten on famously, so different from the angry family relationships some of Sharon's friends reported. They had even taken family vacations. She and Vince had given them a wonderful fiftieth anniversary party and bed-and-breakfast coupons for Michigan. *Why aren't these memories enough for mother?* Sharon tightened her grip on the phone.

She watched as Vince pointed out D'Angelo and Sons down the street. Livy expressed pleasure, standing on her tiptoes for a better view. Sharon needed to press her mother for information since the time for talk was now short. She interrupted Betty's happy litany of her suitors.

"Mom, I wanted to ask you about someone from Chicago that you might know."

"Oh?"

"People named Graves, I believe."

"Who dear? Did you say the name? The street is very noisy here. Say it again." Betty pressed the phone to her ear in hopes she had heard wrong.

"Graves, or something like that."

"What makes you ask?"

Her mother had paused a fraction too long, it seemed to Sharon. She watched Vince tell the girl something more, and he nodded vigorously as he rubbed his face with his hand, a gesture of worry. "Oh, the name just popped into my head, Mom. I wondered why." Sharon tried to sound disinterested.

"Your father and I associated with a few city people. You know, a yearly dinner with men and their wives from the company headquarters. Maybe one couple had a name like that." Her mother prattled on brightly about the past, her suitors forgotten.

"I've got to drop off pastries for the pastors in a few minutes. I'd better go, Mom."

"Me too. Bye."

Sharon was too busy watching Livy out front to ponder the unusual lapse in her mother's etiquette—almost an escape from the phone, with no *Be careful* or *Love you, dear.*

Sharon saw the girl look uncertainly, almost fearfully, toward the front window of Sharon's Desserts and wondered if she had been too cold to her last night. Vince gestured she should go in, and he drove off. The shop door opened gently.

"Hi! Thanks for letting me stay on your sofa bed, Mrs. D'Angelo. Hope you don't mind that I borrowed some shampoo." Her short hair had life to it now, and the pink forelocks slipped from behind her ear and fell over her eye predictably so that she did a little sweeping, flipping, or blowing every few seconds.

"Did my husband show you the cereal I set out?" Sharon could think of nothing friendlier to say.

"I made us some French toast. Hope that was okay."

"Of course." Though of course it wasn't. Maybe she meant Vince made the toast. The counters and stove were probably a mess now.

As she had last night in the kitchen, Livy made a path around the shop, touching things that interested her. She made noises of approval and catechized without waiting for answers. She straightened a chair and ended her survey at the cinnamon rolls.

"Is the glaze almond?"

"Vanilla." Sharon wondered if this was a criticism. "The pastors' breakfast has a standing order for these every month."

She and the girl stared at each other across the flat white boxes ready for delivery at the Presbyterian community hall. Sharon debated whether to ask the girl to ride along or to leave her in the shop, but she hardly knew this person. Sending her to D'Angelo and Sons to wait would give her opportunity to tell her crazy story over there. Taking her along on the delivery was best.

When they pulled up in front of the church, a construction dumpster sat at the drop-off zone. Sharon idled, deciding what to do.

"I'll take them in. No problem." The girl jumped out of the car, balancing the two boxes without a slipup.

Sharon only had time to yell, "I'll do the setup." It took a few minutes to find a parking spot because apparently the meeting had started early. She regretted not confirming the time yesterday. Inside, it was apparent they had changed the meeting location too.

"Sharon, we're in here," someone signaled from an unfamiliar office.

She found the group already gathering around the coffeemaker. Livy had opened the boxes and was using forks to expertly pull apart the rolls. She set them on plates and handed them around, the movement requiring charming flips of her pink forelock.

Sharon folded up the boxes as the group chatted about their kids who were in college, and Livy explained she was in her freshman year. Wishing to discourage more conversation, Sharon moved to the door and was thanked by the Presbyterian pastor who added, "What nice service your niece gave us today, Sharon. She must be quite a help."

"Yes. She keeps me hopping." Sharon hoped this was a noncommittal sort of reply. Inside, she was seething, and on the way to the car, she gave no appreciation to Livy for her help. The girl had some nerve introducing herself that way, Sharon thought.

"Hey, don't be mad at me, Mrs. D'Angelo."

Sharon glanced over at her passenger but the girl's expression was hidden by pink hair.

"I didn't say we were related. That guy just thought so."

"I suppose. You are the right age."

They drove the rest of the way in silence, Sharon thinking Livy's hair, tight jeans, and short top in no way spoke to a similarity suggesting kinship. Her morning conversation with her mother had been no help with this mystery, so she would have to wring more details from the girl.

There was no time for a serious talk when they got back to the shop. She had an order for a flan for pickup at five and the cupcake display needed filling in. They were made but not frosted. Sharon debated where to start.

"I can do that for you. Where's the icing?" Livy grabbed one of the paisley aprons and waved around a narrow spatula.

Maybe the girl could at least frost—or ice—without causing much damage. As Sharon watched the pink-haired sprite tangle herself in the apron with its crisscross shoulder bib, buttons, and ties, she wondered, *What would Mother think?*

"Here, miss, let me." Her name still caught on Sharon's tongue, as if it would confirm her claims.

Livy swirled icing as directed and then hovered over Sharon while she made the flan, asking so many questions that Sharon willingly narrated each step and showed her how to break eggs properly. It felt like the old pre-shop days of demonstrating at home parties where she sold utensils.

The public drama of a tall chocolate soufflé or release of a complex mold was a rush she missed these days.

While they worked on the flan midday, a man in his midforties in an open-collared blue shirt drank coffee leisurely and ate the last cinnamon roll. When Sharon eased the flan in the oven, explaining the temperature to her rapt companion, the man approached the counter.

"Sharon? Phil Krueger, WBEQ South Bend." He presented his card and offered his hand.

"I spotted you at the Lauerbach engagement party last night. Excellent desserts, very creative. And that Italian assistant who lit the Bananas Foster? Just the right staging."

"Thank you." She was about to say Vince was just her husband but remembered her promise to be more professional and added, "It was a pleasure to work with the Lauerbachs."

"Possibly! Lila's kind of a witch." Krueger seemed to wait for agreement. Sharon refrained. "Anyway, I'm looking for new talent for *Indiana Cooks*. You familiar with the show? Taped in Chicago for Midwest Cable."

Sharon heard Livy's gasp and enthused remark behind her. "Ooh, I love that show."

Sharon addressed Krueger. "Yes, I try to catch all the episodes." She kept her tone neutral in spite of her interest.

"I've gotten a feel for you by sitting here. One of the auditioning chefs dropped out of the upcoming tryout. Would you like to step into the opening?"

"I don't have experience with television." Anxiety and hope left Sharon short of words. "But I'd love to hear—"

"Mrs. D'Angelo is very modest." Livy came around the counter. "You should see how beautiful her napoleons are, soooo flaky. She can cook up a storm, believe me."

How the girl invented half-truths with such license and sincerity struck Sharon as a worthwhile skill and perhaps one already applied in last night's family tale.

Krueger acknowledged the compliments and explained the nature of the competition. If Sharon wavered, Livy jumped in with an accolade, until Sharon accepted the offer and shook hands with Krueger again. He wished her luck and left.

Sharon's heart raced at the unbelievable opportunity. The usual path to a television audition had sounded impossible for her: cooking demos at county fairs, videos on social media, and posting a blog and acquiring thousands of friends on her Facebook page. None of this had she done so far, and here opportunity had fallen into her lap as a result of putting up with Lila Lauerbach.

Livy did a little happy dance, drawing a willing Sharon into a twirl.

"Aren't you just dying with excitement, Aunt, Mrs. D'Angelo?"

"I guess you never know what a day will bring," Sharon said to discourage hysterics, then realized she sounded like her mother.

They became preoccupied with the serious business of removing the flan from the pan. Livy quieted down and stood ready to listen to the steps Sharon listed as essential for removal of the flan, creamy yellow under its glaze that was clear as burnt-sugar stained glass.

"Oooh, I wish it was for us!" Livy said as Sharon packed the flan into a to-go box that would be picked up before five.

"Here, as my assistant, you get the drippings." Sharon handed her a wooden spoon and the deep pan where the remaining glaze made a crackled finish. The girl's ecstasy wasn't faked, as Sharon knew from the moans the sugary goo drew out of Vince when he was around to land the prize.

10

Sell, Sell, Sell

As Sharon was encountering the second surprise visitor in less than twenty-four hours, Vince was stopping at the D'Angelo and Sons office to pick up some kitchen design brochures. His mother had beeped him to say that she had scheduled him with Lila Lauerbach, though he protested that the woman must hardly be recovered from the engagement party the night before. And he wasn't very alert because of the time spent with their midnight visitor. He considered canceling, but this was not D'Angelo and Sons' style. In the parking lot, he was ten minutes into a short nap to rally when his mother knocked on the panel truck window.

"Son, you gotta be there on time. One o'clock, sharp." She peered in, the jewels on her new glasses glinting.

He followed the clacking of her fashion boots into the office to pick up the brochures. Her new appearance made him ill at ease. When his father was alive, she shuffled around the house in baggy dresses, black stockings, and worn flats, ostensibly just cooking and cleaning, but in truth, Vince knew with a firm hand she was running "her boys" as she called them—his father, Mike, himself, even their wives when possible. Now a widow, his mother was a new woman who drove a teal Caddy, a trade-in for their maroon Chevy. Her thick hair, returned to a deep brown, swooped from her widow's peak to inches below her ears that now had gold baubles instead of tiny crosses.

"No stopping for fries." She looked him over. "You find something else to wear too."

"Mustard stain?" Vince pulled his shirt out for a look.

"No. You just got to dress up some."

"For who?" Vince looked toward the coffeepot where a jelly donut sat on a napkin.

"Our clients! Women. Look, I've been watching those shows on TV."

"What shows?"

"Vincie. The shows where *bam, bam, bam* they make over a house." Her earrings trembled.

"We don't operate that way."

"I'm meaning the guys who do the talking. They look, how to say it, like hotties. Good in a tool belt. Women like a *mascalzone*."

He could only guess at the exact translation, but her idea was clear. "So I should load up my tool belt to give estimates?" He smirked at his mother.

"And a shirt with open neck. Like this." She flattened the collar open on his polo.

"Ma. It's not disco dancing."

"You were always my handsome son, Vincenzo." She put her hands on his face, then patted his gut. "You're letting yourself go. Be more, more *provocante*." She made a gesture of enticement.

He knew what his mother meant. He was getting a little soft, so he left the lone doughnut.

"And Vincie, a new look is good for the bedroom too. You'll feel better and so will Sharon." Her gold earrings flashed a wink as she used the heel of a boot to make a quick turn toward her desk.

On this astonishing review, he fled to his van in fear she had more to say.

In spite of his mother's advice, he refused to go home and change but was willing to make one concession. *Didn't that friendly guy on the show about dirty jobs—didn't he always wear a hat?* When he pulled in at the Lauerbachs', he found a hat in the jumble behind the seat. Lila met him just as he put it on.

"Vincenzo! I didn't realize you would be coming."

"Call me Vince." He strode toward her front door but not fast enough to escape her squeezing his arm. "Let's take a look at your kitchen. You tell me what you have in mind." When he reviewed the afternoon later, he regretted that phrase.

The arrival of a customer diverted Sharon's attention from worrying about the audition. The man asked for a half dozen peanut butter cookies and inspected the cupcakes.

"What do you have special for Mother's Day?"

"We do a very pretty cake," Sharon said, showing him some laminated photos. "We personalize with her name, of course."

"That's a possibility. Kind of big though. Well, I'll get back to you on that."

"How about a gift basket for breakfast in bed?" Livy said. The laminated photos flipped like playing cards from Sharon's hands.

"I was thinking about a gift for my mother. But breakfast in bed would tickle my kids to give Mommy."

"Are your kids little?"

Sharon watched as Livy negotiated ages and favorite breakfast foods, referring to her own foibles in gift giving to her mother that included a new floor mop. The young father and Livy laughed freely.

"So, how about we include a half dozen muffins in a real basket, tucked into a country-style cotton napkin stenciled with 'All Our Love'? We can add breakfast tea, if you like."

At the mention of the stenciled message, Sharon ended her pretense of sponging the counter.

"What will this set me back?" The man got out his credit card. Sharon sprang to life in the longish silence and did some quick figures, including a guess for the basket, napkin, and tea.

Sharon smiled and said, "That will be thirty dollars with a pickup late Saturday afternoon to assure freshness. Or how about home delivery on Sunday? Five dollar delivery fee?"

Ready to propose anything to equal Livy's salesman-ship, Sharon suggested this final touch. Let Vince complain now about her customer service. In fact, he could do delivery on Mother's Day. And he would be happy to as penance for the dreaded, endless Mother's Day celebration at the D'Angelos'. Even the girl looked impressed, Sharon noted with satisfaction.

"Livy, please describe our muffin choices from this list."

Sharon wrote up the sales, ran his credit card, and thanked him with a professional smile. As soon as the shop door closed, she turned to Olivia.

"The profit margin on the basket is pretty good, right?" Livy said.

"Depending on where I'm going to get a basket, tea, and a napkin with stenciling!" Sharon tapped her fingers on the counter.

"If we could just stop by a craft store—you have one here, right?—I'll have a half dozen setups by midnight tonight. Breakfast baskets could be a big item for us, uh you, for the holiday."

"Yes, Elkhart has a craft store, two in fact. And I'm sure you can have setups whipped up by midnight. But that's beside the point."

"So you don't like the idea?"

"The point is—" Sharon wasn't sure what. The girl had proposed a sterling idea she hadn't thought of herself, as well as proposed that they were related. Before she could finish her sentence, Sharon saw a flicker of uncertainty before the pink hair covered Livy's face.

"I understand I might not be welcome here, considering. So I can go anytime you say." Livy took a long look around.

"You have baskets to make for Mother's Day, remember?" Sharon practiced a look that reminded offspring of forgotten algebra assignments. "Let's figure out a sign advertising the Mother's Day special event."

"I can do a whole social media campaign." Livy pulled her hair into a topknot with a rubber band and smiled. "Can I use that laptop?"

11

An Invitation and an Acknowledgement

*B*etty's day turned out to be more productive and livelier than she had expected. After her polite one-line email to fisherman Ed Conley, he proposed that he take her to the InterContinental Hotel for dinner that very night.

"I thought this would just be lunch," Betty said, studying the email with Eleanor.

"Apparently he's anxious to treat you like a lady. That's a very swanky hotel for dinner." Eleanor was always ready to jump right in no matter the circumstances, especially when it was a risk on someone else's account, Betty noticed.

"But so soon? Tonight?" Betty scanned the attached photo of Ed in a pork pie hat and holding a fly rod.

"Why wait? He figures you won't be any younger by next week." Eleanor poked Betty and enlarged the photo to look him over better. His smile grew, as did his hearing aids and fishing gear.

"His rod looks sturdy," Eleanor said.

"Charlie had one for trout."

"You've never said much about Charlie's rod."

"The subject's never—Oh, for heaven's sake, Eleanor." Betty's embarrassment was a passing cloud. They laughed until they were gulping for air.

Analysis then flew about the speed of the invitation. He was rather presumptuous in assuming she had nothing on the calendar for the evening. But perhaps this haste was a measure of his sincere interest? Though she had not anticipated dating so quickly, Betty needed a distraction from Sharon's question about someone named Graves. *It was awfully close to Graveswell,* she thought. Some latent childhood memory might be intruding in Sharon's busy mind, something loosed by stress or coincidence, perhaps. Would she worry it bulldog-like, or let it go? Knowing her daughter, she felt the former seemed likely, and where that path led, Betty was sure disillusionment lay.

None of this concern was she ready to discuss with Eleanor, so accepting Ed's offer was in her best interest. Hunched over the laptop and after a storm of deletes, Betty typed, "Greetings Ed, Thank you very much for the dinner invitation. I am free tonight."

"Add, 'as it happens,'" Eleanor said. "He should feel fortunate you can accept."

Betty added the suggestion though it sounded a little snooty and composed the next sentence after a swoop into the thesaurus. "I would be happy to meet you in the InterContinental lobby at six thirty. You asked about my dinner preference. Beef tips au jus, rice almondine, and chocolate mousse sound sumptuous."

"Why does he need your dinner order? That seems tacky." Eleanor reached over to scroll to his message.

"Maybe he has a coupon," Betty said ignoring her friend's huff of "even tackier" and returning to her reply. She decided to add a line that hinted at the nature of social contact she expected on a first date. "I look forward to hearing more about your hobbies and family."

She typed her name before Eleanor could suggest more revision and pressed Send, wondering if Ed would think to check his mail throughout the day. It was early afternoon already. However, before she and Eleanor had finished a second cup of tea, he had replied with rather excessive enthusiasm, including his photo again to avoid confusion over identity, he said.

"Maybe I should write back saying I'll be wearing a yellow rose."

"Oh no." Eleanor closed the laptop. "Being somewhat incognito will give you the upper hand. If he looks unbalanced, you can slip out before he spots you."

"I'm sure Mr. Conley will be a pleasant dinner companion for beef tips au jus. Besides, *boeuf au jus*," Betty had pursed her lips for the pronunciation, "will give me a chance to practice my French."

"If only it were *boeuf à la Bourguignon*." Eleanor accentuated the *r*, then rolled her eyes as Betty reopened the laptop and clacked away on the keyboard.

"I wonder how you say the 'tips' part." Betty scrolled through several pages with no success. "Oh, well. I'll stick with *boeuf au jus*."

"The phrase 'French speaker' did not occur to me when I met Ed Conley at speed dating, Betty."

"Okay, okay. I just like being in the know these days." Betty studied the list of French words related to dining. Chocolate mousse must be there somewhere.

"Don't scare him off with your erudition."

"Actually, I thought he'd be scared off by your address if he picked me up here in a cab the way he offered."

"Well, even the *grande dames* of Lake Shore Drive like to meet new men—and their rods."

"I'm going to just ignore you for the rest of the afternoon." Betty put her nose in the air with a sniff. "Besides, I need to steam my new sweater. There's a fold in it."

"You can ask Rosa to do it."

Betty still couldn't get used to home help and so rummaged around for the iron, probably giving the housekeeper extra work in the end. Then she sat in a comfortable chair, rested her head in a way so as to not muss her hair styled just yesterday, and took a fortifying, pre-date nap. Fortunately she wasn't clairvoyant. The end-of-the-afternoon tête-à-tête in Elkhart did not enter her dreams.

Though the spring light belied the hour, it was closing time at Sharon's Desserts. Since the gift basket discussion, Sharon had been busy with ordering baking supplies. She worked at her small desk that was a rat's nest of lists, clippings, phone numbers, sticky notes, and bills. This was a task she disliked, and one she wasn't very good at, and the physical jumble further disordered her concentration. *Doing* was her strong point—baking, inventing, and instructing and the details therein were where she shone. She had been a hit at home parties with recipe demos of high-end utensils and cookware. These days she was surprised how much of the other sorts of things from her weak points Sharon's Desserts required.

Livy kept busy refolding the dish towels, trying on the aprons, and adjusting the chairs and tables, all the while flipping her pink mane behind her ear. This animation distracted Sharon from her orders and caused her to wonder whether Vince may have gotten personal information from her, though he hadn't stopped by or called. She slapped down her pencil. *We need to get that girl back to Chicago,* she thought. Apparently, she went to college, so she had somewhere to go back to.

After Livy rehung the last apron, Sharon saw her reach for the handsome photo of her father on the shelf above the hooks. In her haste to rescue the picture, Sharon knocked her hip hard against the counter. She took the photo from Livy and set it back on the shelf farther from the edge.

"Sorry!" Livy drew out the word. "I just wanted to look at it up close."

"It's very fragile."

The two faced off in front of the aprons, a line of reproachful grannies who sent Sharon the reminder that honey catches more flies than vinegar. Wilting, she made some conciliatory gestures, pulling out chairs so they could sit.

"Now, let's go over your story from last night about the Graves. Am I getting the name right?" Sharon tried to sound conversational.

"It's Graves*well.*"

"And who are you in this exactly?"

"I'm pretty sure I'm your niece." The girl flashed a brilliant smile.

In her heart Sharon already knew who the girl was. She had seen it in the girl's quirky, uneven smile, in the tapered fingers so like the ones that had built a canopy bed for Sharon's own tenth birthday, and most of all in the blue eyes that sloped downward at the edges. "Miles family eyes," her dad had called them, eyes that she herself didn't inherit but that gave Livy's face its wistfulness.

Sharon crossed her arms and sat back. "I'm still surprised you're here without even calling us at least." She thought of the phone calls with no one speaking. "Or you did call, didn't you?"

Livy shrugged, then spoke in a tone suggesting all was now perfectly clear. "Like I said last night"—Sharon refrained from interjecting *as, not like*—"I really appreciate the money from my grandpa. Your dad." She gestured toward the prize photo and went on. "You and Uncle Vince have been really nice too, just like I figured. Not at all like what my family said."

"What did they say?" Sharon couldn't hide her interest.

"Well, finding out your dad was uh, a player, you know, you might not want—"

This had to stop. Sharon came to the point.

"Look, Olivia, we don't have extra money to help you out more, even if we are related. And I still think it's *if.*" She shouldn't acknowledge to the kinship claim so fast. Surely the family wanted money.

"Yeah, I know that, but that's not why I came."

"Then what? What do you want?"

"You don't have kids do you? I didn't see any photos in your house."

This observation rankled. Sharon snapped, "That's not really your business. But no, we don't."

"Grandma Irene said you don't have any brothers or sisters either. And neither do I, by the way. Not that you've asked."

Sharon pictured these people with their horrible name making a steely analysis of the Miles-D'Angelo family to the extent that the girl as single heir had her eye on the whole estate. What other gossip about them had been passed around the Graveswell dinner table?

"This discussion is over, Olivia. But we will help you get back to Chicago, of course." Even if the girl was who she said she was, there was little need for an extended visit.

Livy began to sob with her head down on the café table so that her hair covered her face. Sharon's previous job as a hospital social worker had not required working with young people. She was unsure what to do, but one angle occurred to her.

"Are you in trouble?"

"No, I don't hook up." Livy shook her head violently.

Sharon had read about this inexplicably casual activity. "So, maybe something else is bothering you. Boyfriend? Drugs? Divorce?" What other things upset girls? Sharon wasn't sure.

"I'm not doing drugs. I have a great boyfriend, and my parents' divorce was a long time ago. Again, not that you asked, Mrs. D'Angelo."

Livy stood up and put on her jacket. "I just wanted to know the truth about who I am. But you don't seem to get that. Maybe my family was right after all that you wouldn't want to meet us." She left the shop, closing the door with a whoosh.

To Sharon, the burst of air seemed to come from a newly opened window, one that looked out on the vista of a strange landscape. Natives scurried below, with histories that had twined with the Miles family unbeknownst to her and surely to her mother. What were they doing down there—what had they done, and what would they do in the future? To protect her mother, she needed to keep track of these countrymen.

Livy, her niece presumably, sat outside on the step, head on her knees. Sharon, tingling with a sense of she-didn't-know-what, found she wanted to put her arm around the crumpled figure and rock the two of them, providing comfort against the perils of this new territory. She locked the shop. Livy looked up.

"I'd better figure out a way to get back to Chicago. Maybe the bus?" She began to consult her phone.

"Amtrak goes there every morning, Livy. Why don't you stay with us again tonight?" She hadn't meant to be so cold before. "The couch is still made up. Let's go home."

"Oh, thanks, really." Livy threw her arms around Sharon. "And there are the gift baskets and napkins to get. Remember?"

Sharon took a long split second to ease out of the embrace. "Oh yes. And we'll have to tell your Uncle Vince about the cooking show audition."

"OMG, he's going to be surprised."

"That's an understatement."

It seemed only fair that Vince should have a surprise too, one like hers, not entirely welcome.

12

A Free Dinner with Strings Attached

At six thirty Betty stepped out of a cab on Michigan Avenue and was swept through the gold doors of the InterContinental hotel. Before she even got her bearings in the lobby, she felt her arm taken in a hearty grip as Ed Conley welcomed her happily. His plaid sports coat was a contrast to the somber tones worn by other men standing around, but it had been so long ago that madras was in, perhaps it was back. Ed might be just ahead of the fashion revival, or perhaps more likely, Betty thought, this whole date thing was just as ill chosen as the jacket. She wilted in the glamor of the gold staircase and marble floor—a very fancy place for a first date. Ed too was scanning the lobby uncertainly.

"Ah-ha!" he said, apparently finding a missing clue. "Here we are. This way."

He pointed toward the elevators, though Betty noticed the restaurant was in the other direction. Perhaps he had dishonest intentions. Repressing her disquiet, she pretended confidence in the crowd of well-dressed people, draping Eleanor's lavish paisley shawl on her new pink sweater. She introduced pleasantries about the weather with Ed as they waited for an elevator.

"You look very nice, Betty," he said when the door closed. She let the shawl fall open a bit more, wondering if dating etiquette required a reciprocal comment on his jacket.

When the doors opened, Ed said, "We're looking for the Hall of Lions and the Camelot Room."

Sure enough, they could see lion embellishments and couples wandering along with champagne glasses and gold-rimmed plates. *Maybe we're going to a buffet,* Betty thought. As they approached a room called Camelot, they could hear jazz.

"This must be it." Ed took her arm.

Betty could see Ed's relief that the elevator ride and the corridor of lions had not been a wild goose chase. At the Camelot Room stood a gold lettered sign flanked by sharply dressed personnel in black. They held nosegays they presented to female guests.

"Oh my, thank you." Betty found it was a wristlet.

An attractive young man held her shawl as she slipped on the flowers. He offered Ed a gift pen and shook his hand firmly, saying, "Welcome to Leisure Living Time Shares—your homes away from home."

"Oh boy. I knew this would be swanky," Ed said in a stage whisper to Betty who had tried to draw back from the door after the official welcome. He went on, "Live jazz, champagne, the red-carpet treatment. Let's go sign in."

"Is this a restaurant?" Betty again hesitated.

"A banquet room. When I saw this offer at the Inter-Continental, I signed up as a couple, last minute. Drinks and dinner, the works." Ed beamed at Betty.

"But they want to sell us a timeshare."

"We just have to watch a few slides. Don't worry." He patted her back. "I've studied all the angles. This is the way to get a great meal at a high-class hotel."

And a free one for a date, Betty thought, but her resistance was weakened by the yummy aromas, the music, and the escape from the alarming Hall of Lions, most appropriate, she told Eleanor later, for the gauntlet of salespeople that welcomed them and led them to the registration table. The purpose of the gift pen was obvious once they approached the table.

"We could each use our own names, Betty, if you'd prefer," Ed said, apparently waffling over whether she was angry about his posing them as a married couple.

Betty wondered if he realized they were an incongruous pair—Ed in a madras jacket with a Petoskey stone tie clip on a fish print tie and white buck shoes she hadn't seen since the fifties, and her in a pink Eileen Fisher sweater that had cost a shocking amount. It was a birthday surprise from Eleanor. At her throat was her gold pendant from Charlie, purchased in anticipation of their sixtieth wedding anniversary but delivered posthumously. She had put this on only after Eleanor's final appraisal of her appearance. Why she chose it, she couldn't say, other than it was lovely and a familiar talisman for this unexplored territory.

Ed looked desperate to please. She reassured him, "Ed, I'm sure no one will be shocked if we use our own names."

As they waited in line, her musings returned. Fortunately, Sharon and Vince married before moving in together so that she and Charlie hadn't had to adjust their attitude toward pre-marital households. These days white wedding dresses were symbolic of the purity of matrimonial intentions only, and bridesmaids, or brides, might waddle along the aisle eight months pregnant. With the wisdom of age, Betty could see trying out a relationship had its merits. Perhaps Eleanor wouldn't have needed three tries at marriage had she lived with any of the candidates first, but her husbands was one topic Eleanor refused to discuss.

Ed fingered the Petoskey stone on his tie clip, still anxious over the registration and the name difficulty. Their turn was next. He broke into Betty's musing on the state of marriage.

"Of course, it could be that you kept your own name in marriage, especially if you're a physician," Ed said. "Hey, I'll bet Dr. Joyce Brothers wasn't married to a Mr. Brothers." He winked. "Remember her?"

He got out his phone to confirm the name of the noted relationship doctor, but Betty interrupted his research.

"Actually I'd choose to be a lady PhD. I've heard they keep their own names." She went on to explain that farmers' daughters didn't often go to college in her time despite their aptitude and desire. "I might have been a history scholar, Dr. Elizabeth Montgomery. Who knows?"

Ed stepped up to the table hesitantly. Betty watched a woman with orange hair take in his jacket and treat him as an interloper here for the free food. As she offered him the investment folder with a limp hand, Betty felt her liking for her date rise measurably. Assuming the real object of their presence was free food seemed an unfair condemnation. These salespeople were equally devious, advertising a simple presentation for edification when it was obvious to even an ingénue that this outfit intended *to give them the business.* Attendees, Betty surmised, wouldn't be escaping without a thorough drubbing on the investment opportunities of timeshares, with remonstrance to those who wavered. She wasn't the widow of an insurance salesman with nothing to show for it.

Betty took firmly the folder offered lamely to Ed, much to his surprise. "I'll handle this—Pookie," Betty said nudging Ed.

He smiled radiantly. The orange-haired woman moved them to a highboy for writing. Betty refrained from saying "thank you," possibly for the first time in her life.

Heads together over the folder, they found the basic info pages. "Go ahead, Betty, you fill it out." Ed handed her the gold pen. "It says 10 karat!" He squinted to read the brand name.

With another representative hovering, Betty wrote each of their names in her pretty script. Then with her hand on Ed's arm, she said loudly, "Let's give our Chicago address since we're here until July."

"Yes, dear." Ed bobbed his head. Betty printed Eleanor's address, with the numerals reversed, turning the paper so the words "Lake Shore Drive" jumped out at the sales rep.

"For our dream location, how about Fiji?" Betty was sure this was pretty darn expensive for a timeshare, as well as far away.

"And the Gulf Coast for deep sea fishing." Ed looked at an array of getaway locations on large video screens. His expression was rapt at the scenes of cruisers with trolling lines.

Betty obediently checkmarked Venice, adding aloud to the rep, "We're tired of St. Pete." He made a forced nod.

After demurring about identifying the range for their incomes and ages with a shrug—invasive, identity theft, et cetera, et cetera—they turned in their paperwork, filled out the door prize tickets, and were more than ready for the dinner.

"Wow, you're really in the game, Betty." Ed locked her hand through his arm to move toward a quieter spot. "I had no idea we would be pressured like this. Not at all like seminars on wills and trusts or diabetes education." He inched the tie clip down a bit to loosen his collar. Betty resisted giving the tie a straighten-up afterward.

She wondered how often he took women to these sorts of free offerings for life events from cradle to grave. She wasn't sure whether to be insulted, because, after all, she had chosen to wear a memento from her late husband on a first date. At the moment she was famished, so Ed's intentions and their duplicity were forgotten.

She felt his guiding hand again as he said, "Let's get some horse's ovaries. I'm starving."

"Pardon?"

"Horse's ovaries." Betty's smile was faint. *Did he mean hors d'oeuvres?*

He moved them toward a waiter holding a tray of stuffed mushrooms that was soon proffered grandly. The correct pronunciation of *boeuf au jus* seemed unnecessary once Ed's meaning was clear.

"After you, Betty," Ed said handing her a tiny plate.

Soon they accepted second glasses of champagne and various tidbits from other trays, and then surveyed the competition for the door prizes. Most of the couples were fiftyish, many, they guessed, looking for investments to hedge against inflation. The younger couples might see a timeshare as a good way to get a family vacation. And there were a few couples in their age range, but most not as mobile as they were.

"Let's take a look at the prize list," Betty said, finding a bright pink page in the sales folder. "First prize, five nights in a three-bedroom timeshare in St. John, US Virgin Islands," she read. "My goodness! That's quite a prize."

"Have you been to the Caribbean?"

"I hardly know where it is. Except south." She read on, describing the second prize, a four-day cruise for two, and third, a two-night stay at a Manhattan hotel. Lastly were four vouchers toward rates on a Florida timeshare.

"No prizes of a vacation in Philly?" Ed grinned.

"First prize, one night in Philadelphia." Betty pretended to announce grandly.

"Second prize, two nights," Ed kept up the routine.

"Third prize, three nights!" They spoke in unison and laughed.

"I'd love to go to Philadelphia, actually." Betty described patriotic highlights and Ed added a ballpark.

"I have a good feeling about these prize odds, Betty." He patted her hand. "Maybe we'll reel in a big one." His hand flew from hers to the Petoskey stone to make another adjustment.

On her side, Betty was having a somewhat bad feeling. Was the price of a free dinner a week in the Caribbbean with this man from Mayberry? She glanced around, estimating the guests to be about two hundred, making their chances, what, one in two hundred? *No, better than that.* One ticket had been provided to each twosome. *One in a hundred.* She fanned herself with her napkin.

On their search for dinner seating, Ed said, "I'm with you on the *boeuf*, Betty. Sorry the beef tips, that is." He spoke with a perfect accent as far as she could tell.

"You speak French?

"Not really. I just like to show off a little. 'Horse's ovaries' was an old family joke. My mother did speak French. My dad and us kids would drive her nuts with mispronunciations."

Betty laughed then took up the subject of her French class, asking for help on words she had learned. "It's so nice to feel in the know at a concert or museum or ordering wine," she said.

"I guess I don't do much of those things," Ed replied.

Betty felt guilty about referring to these artsy pursuits. After all, she was recently only from Elkhart with no need to show off.

With the intention of putting folks in the mood for timesharing, the organizers set the tables for six. Ed led them to a table with a husband and wife and two sisters. The woman in the couple barely spoke, they observed soon, and the two sisters were in a war of silence with each other, asking tablemates to pass dishes that were clearly closest to the other sister. It was hard to imagine the siblings sharing a vacation condo. Perhaps they too had signed up just for the free dinner. Fortunately for everyone, Ed broke the awkward silences with a fish story for each course.

Before dessert, the sales team geared up for the presentation. Lights dimmed, and a jocular man in his early fifties took the microphone. After an opening quip, he began to work his way through the dangers of inflation to any nest egg the guests might be incubating. As he moved on to vacation homes as security, Ed whispered, "Let's step out, Betty." His hand under her arm seemed extra-solicitous as they slipped out. He made some dramatic gestures at the doorway patting his chest but waving off a sales team member.

"Do you need help, Ed? Are you all right?" Betty looked for a chair.

"I always skip the presentation. A little heart trouble gesture gets me out." He pantomimed restricted breathing. "They don't want a fuss. But let's go back for the drawing in about forty minutes. Once, I won a full-body massage with a team of Swedish therapists. They surely knew how to relax your sore spots."

"How nice." Betty refused to picture it.

Ed suggested a stakeout for the wait, a white couch on the mezzanine. Here his patience as a fisherman paid off since Betty found he was as content as she was trolling the lobby. They analyzed the May-December couples in particular. A wife had been exchanged for a newer model, Betty guessed. Or could that be a daughter? Though he didn't wish to shock her, Ed said, he guessed some could be escorts, particularly the showy ones.

"Really, and in such a nice place!" Betty took a second look at the last couple where the woman in a backless dress teetered in spangled heels. Her flush-faced companion nosed her ear while he guided her along. Clearly, they were not a gentleman and lady, a couple to describe later to Eleanor.

When Ed excused himself for a restroom trip, Betty fell into contemplation. *Had Charlie been here?* A time machine might show him in his favorite grey suit leading Irene Graveswell in a black dress to the restaurant. Charlie, his good manners part of his effective salesmanship and appeal to women, would have taken her hand, putting himself first to make their way in the crowd.

In contrast, Betty couldn't picture Charlie and herself as a couple here. Recalling her middle years, she saw a plain, motherly woman. Sharon's braces, flute lessons, Girl Scout trip money, and college savings were their daily concerns. No, it would have been irresponsible to spend on city clothes, hotels, or fancy meals, according to Charlie. She had held up her end of thrift and a sensible lifestyle. She kept her full-length winter coat good for years by wearing it Sundays only. For ordinary days, there was the old coat on a closet hook. Yes, for the Elks club dinners she had a couple of dressy outfits, and Charlie's attentions told her she looked *good enough*. But now she wished to turn back the clock. Had her zealous practicality driven him elsewhere? Would he have brought her here instead of Irene if she had made demands for a more interesting marriage? Her sacrifices may have discounted his masculinity and not kept the home fires bright enough. Perhaps she herself had been the root of his restlessness? It was a weight on her heart.

Ed, oblivious to his askew belt, made his way back to her. It was time to go back for the drawing. Betty considered pleading she had a headache, but it seemed unfair given his obvious pleasure in the evening and her company. They arrived just in time to hear, "Ed Conley and Betty Miles. Ed and Betty? Where are you? Pack your bags for the Big Apple!"

Ed waved wildly. "Over here. Here we are!" He gave the Petoskey stone a jerk and grabbed Betty's hand as they were led to the front of the room. She couldn't help her own enthusiasm, hugging Ed and even a sales team member just like women on the *Price Is Right*.

It was only during the cab ride home that she pondered the social implications of this prize that would require seeing him again a few times and playing roommate—or more—on a trip to New York City. Would these activities make them "an item"? It was definitely something to discuss with Eleanor. Possibly Sharon. She'd have to gauge her daughter's mood.

13

Compromising Positions

D inner at the D'Angelos' was a quiet affair compared to Betty's evening at the InterContinental. Everyone treaded lightly, with many thank-yous and offers for clearing up. Sharon shared in an off-hand way the news about the television show, downplaying the possibility of success while Livy asserted that she would ace it. Vince wondered where it would take place and what happened next if she won. Sharon could answer neither question.

After a simple dessert of fruit, Sharon moved like a dreamer through the familiar landscape of her kitchen. She loaded the dishwasher and while handwashing a platter nearly dropped it. One of the final china pieces from Betty's farm home, the large dish had a sweet scene of cows that Sharon had loved as a child. Sharon recalled how on Sundays her mother had filled the platter with pot roast or chicken, and Sharon had turned it toward herself to watch for the placid animals as the dish emptied. Tonight the scene struck her with sadness, the cows unaware that their lives were only in human service, their placidity mirroring her own ignorance in light of the recent upheaval in family history.

Livy retired with her phone to the sofa bed, and Vince worked on plans for Lila's kitchen, or seemed to.

Abruptly, Sharon got her keys, purse, and jacket, saying as she headed out, "I forgot something at the shop."

"I'll go with." Vince got up.

"No. I'll only be a few minutes. You need to keep your eye on that girl Livy. Don't let her decide to call my mother next."

The wail of a freight train followed Sharon on her way to the shop. No more had been said about sending her niece—she tried out the phrase aloud in the car—back to Chicago the next morning. Unlocking the door of Sharon's Desserts generally gave her a thrill of proprietorship, no matter her fatigue if she came in early to bake or late to stay at her books.

This time was different.

Her down payment and even the soda fountain tables and chairs that she had carefully picked out came from hush money. The savings bonds assured that if she ever found out about the Graveswells, she would not tell her mother and would forgive her father for his imperfection. She would keep him the shining example of a family man that he had prized so much. She didn't doubt that he had loved her mother and her, that she was his princess, but he had loved someone other than her mother too. And quite clearly another daughter. This disgusted her. And maybe the shop money was an apology too that he hadn't lived up to the highest standard of good husband that he had aspired to. Well, she would accept the bribe and keep this from her mother at all costs. Forgiveness might have to wait.

Sharon detoured on her way home to drive along Main Street where the theater marque was bright with red and yellow lights. Leaving her car by the rail station, she walked to a little park. As she sat on a bench, a freight train rumbled through. At car number seventy-eight, Sharon realized she was counting aloud as if to entertain a kid. Well, now she had a niece, a little old for counting cars or buying Easter dresses, but one who seemed very much to need her and Vince. Livy was a legacy from and for her father, the grandchild he had without a doubt wanted, but Sharon had not provided.

She took an angry turn around the park. Here she was at middle age on the brink of success with her business, and she was still in service to her parents. She would have to soothe, pave the way, lie if necessary, to keep their happy family story intact.

While Sharon was counting train cars, Vince was rough sketching ideas for the Lauerbach kitchen. At the office, his mother's assistant would enter them into a layout program. He knew he should learn to do this himself, sometime when he wasn't busy. For now, he enjoyed the feel of his pencil on graph paper where he could do the scaling without the help of a computer program. He worked up a couple of plans involving moving the fridge to reduce the number of steps between appliances, adding a prep sink to the island, enlarging the windows, and—*What else was it Lila said she wanted?* He chewed his pencil. Little else about the kitchen. Vince recalled his visit.

"I like to get acquainted with people who design for us," Lila said when he arrived as his mother had ordered. "How else could you know what I want?" She led him into the family room where Frank Sinatra's "Come Fly with Me" played softly.

"Can I interest you in a craft beer?" Clearly she was in no hurry to talk about a floor plan.

Perhaps this was part of the new routine expected of TV-style construction people. He accepted a drink, though it wasn't five o'clock anywhere nearby, and she brought a frosty glass complete with a floating slice of orange. Then she clicked on the gas fireplace and pointed to a small leather couch. He removed his tool belt so as not to slash her couch and realized too late the gesture might be seen as suggestive. She sat girlishly with her knees tucked up, putting her very close on the cushions that whispered with every move she made. She spread a kitchen picture book open, but preferred conversation.

"You first, Vince. What moves you?" She smiled. Though moving her fridge was what came to mind, he knew that's not what Lila meant.

"Working in my yard, I guess."

"Oh, a nature lover. I like that in a man."

"About your kitchen. What I'm thinking is first we bring in more light with bigger windows, maybe even French doors." Her hand fell on his thigh when she turned to look toward the kitchen.

"I'd like that very much."

Is she talking about the windows? he wondered. Her enthusiasm seemed overdone for so mundane a suggestion, and her hand lingered long and warm.

"Tell me something you like, Vincenzo."

"Kitchen-wise, we often feature a prep sink. You know, for washing vegetables and—"

"I'd love to have D'Angelo and Sons do the kitchen. But let's get to the point here, Vincenzo." She moved her hand up firmly. *"There's something between us. I felt it last night at the party."*

He had to admit her lithe yoga body was a turn-on, as was her directness. He disliked the way women pussyfooted around instead of just saying what they wanted—where they wanted the stove or what they expected for their birthday. He had always fallen short on gifts and then felt guilt for days after, even though Sharon or his mother said that it doesn't matter at all. And maybe it didn't, but he felt it did. Hell.

"Let's get to know each other. You know you want to." Lila had pouted like a porn star. *"Come here."* She patted the slim space between them on the leather couch.

Sitting at his own kitchen table, Vince shivered remembering the next part. She had yanked off her shirt and pressed her breasts against him. For one long—and delicious—moment he had wavered. What harm would a little touchy-feely do? This was what his mother meant by women liking a rascal. He had googled *mascalzone* to see what was expected. Probably these TV guys or gals (both with abs and ponytails) just waited until the camera went off before shagging the homeowner of the preferred gender. At that pivotal moment on Lila's insinuating couch, his beeper had buzzed with a text, a reminder from his mother to mention the cabinet sale. If she had only known! His mother had saved his marriage and maybe lost them a $50,000 job.

He had patted Lila on the shoulder a few times, told her she was a beautiful woman, and picked up his tool belt and left. But he had whistled in his truck. Yes, he could be *provocante* with no props apparently. The stupid hat, he tossed into the back.

The "Good night, Uncle Vince" called to him by Livy killed another replay. Next, the garage door closing made him cross out some notes about the visit to Lila's where he had printed a compromising phrase. Then, hoping Sharon's trip to the shop had worked a miracle in her mood, he headed for the shower right before she came in the kitchen.

In Eleanor's condo, the lights finally went out about midnight, after Betty had been wrung dry of every detail about her date at the InterContinental. Both ladies concluded Ed had earned many points for originality.

14

A Lesson in Art Appreciation

Several days later, when Betty and Eleanor were strolling through the Cultural Center looking for friends who might want to go to lunch, they saw the door open on a new installation for the artist-in-residence program. The previous month, an artist had hung pages of a graphic novel in progress. Betty and Eleanor had studied the drawings, some cleverly inked but all mystifying in terms of a story line.

"We must be too old for this new stuff," Betty had said.

"It looks like *Li'l Abner* redux to me. That one's Daisy Mae but with spiked hair." Eleanor had waved her cane at a print of a buxom girl in shorts, and then had begun an inquisition about the state of the novel with the artist who was sketching nearby. After fifteen minutes of banter, he had looked to Betty for help in moving along her literary friend.

This month's artist-in-residence, they learned from the welcome poster, was a paper and fiber artist. The bright artworks of various sizes drew the women inside immediately.

"Oh, how intriguing." Eleanor marched up to a wall hanging of blues and greens, and read, *"Mirage*, felted wool." She moved on to admire a shawl covered with birds, a muted background made of felted wool fibers, the birds superimposed in bright colors.

"Now, this is art," Betty said. "I understand this better than last month's." She studied some smaller pieces whose construction she couldn't discern at first.

"Yes, at least you can tell what these are about." Eleanor looked at the shawl again.

"Except I'm not sure about this one, but I can see it's made with layers of paper."

Betty studied a framed object, a dress like one for a large paper doll. She thought of Sharon carefully cutting out paper dresses from the glossy books they bought at Woolworth's or the Betsy McCall figures from *McCall's* magazine. They often worked together, Sharon prattling about what each girl cutout might do in the various clothes. Those had been sweet hours. Betty had cut out the more complicated items since slashing off a sleeve or tab could send Sharon into tears. *You do it, Mommy.* Betty could still hear her daughter's voice and see her hands pressing the page toward her, a forecast of perfectionist tendencies later. Outgrowing Betsy McCall, Sharon had taken the books of older girls or movie stars to her room where Betty was sure she worked out preteen angst with the characters, dressing the paper dolls in strange outfit combinations. *Did girls still play with paper dolls today?* Betty wondered. *Or perhaps this gentle pastime had been co-opted by adults, as had coloring books.*

These dresses by the artist-in-residence were layered, Betty could see. Dress pattern tissue paper, holiday paper, recipes, snippets of silk and dishcloths, and some bits made translucent so all layers were visible at the same time yet had depth. A woman's life summed up—the little dresses charming and alarming at the same time.

"H'um, pretty, I guess," Betty said.

Eleanor looked over her shoulder. "I agree with you, but I'll bet the artist might be disappointed with just 'pretty.' Sounds dismissive, especially since it's a woman artist. Juliette Graveswell. Strange name."

"What's the name?" Betty turned away abruptly from her examination of a sculpture.

"Juliette Graveswell, noted Chicago artist," Eleanor read aloud from the bio, speeding through various awards, galleries, and her teaching at art schools. When Betty didn't respond, Eleanor turned to find her friend looking drained and seated on a bench.

"Graveswell. How common could that name be?" Betty said.

"You know some Graveswells?"

"Eleanor, remember that woman that Charlie left money to? Remember how I met her working at the bank when I opened his lockbox?"

"So—"

"Her name was Graveswell, Irene Graveswell."

"This woman is Juliette. Can't be the same one," Eleanor said, sitting down beside Betty and patting her hand. Then she added, "It could be a sister. Maybe a daughter?" She rested her hand on Betty's again.

"There could be a lot of people with that name in Chicago, Eleanor." Betty shook off her hand and headed toward the door. "I'm starved. Let's find some lunch."

"The sign says the she'll be here from one to three today. We could come back to check her out."

"Oh, why bother?" Betty was looping her scarf for the third time around her neck. "I'm sure there are lots of Graveswells. Chicago's a big place. Her art is pretty, well, skillful, I have to say." Maybe the layered collages were just miscellaneous cloth and paper, but their suggestion of the hidden being visible took her breath away.

The women decided to try out a new café that advertised wholesome breads, soups, and salads. Eleanor enjoyed the waitstaff's description of several specials. "Tomato bisque soup, cinnamon glazed beets, local horseradish chopped on a turkey salad, squash soup with floating artichoke hearts," he said speeding through a list of wholesome choices.

What I'd give for an American cheese sandwich on white bread, Betty thought. Even the cheese being French here was not a distraction from her disturbing thoughts. She held up her hand to stop the recital of the specials. "I'd like the tomato bisque soup. A cup, please."

"With the avocado toast! Good choice." The waiter wrote with a flourish, apparently her order a triumph on his part. Betty grimaced. Avocados would be in cornflakes next.

Actually, she hardly noticed the green spread as she ate. She was thinking of the paper artist and Sharon's out-of-the-blue question about somebody named Graves. She needed to ditch Eleanor, who would be much too inquisitive, and return to the exhibit.

"You go on to Macy's and look for your night cream. I'll meet you at the fountain in forty minutes."

"What are you going to do?" Eleanor set down her coffee cup with a clank.

Betty was swirling the contents of her purse, head down. "I'm going to get some of that fancy popcorn for Vince."

"You're a terrible liar, Betty. You won't see Vince for another week at least. I know where you're going."

"Forty minutes. At the fountain." Betty slapped a twenty on the table—she had become inured to the cost of a Chicago lunch—and marched off at top speed.

Indeed the artist was working at a large table when Betty peeked in the door and then strolled in to examine the artwork. She moved so she could look at a sculpture and beyond it at the artist. The sculpture was a dress that hovered over the armature as if an invisible woman had just shrugged it on, its fine fabric falling in graceful folds. Betty leaned in for a close look.

"My goodness, it's paper."

The artist looked up from her worktable. "Handmade paper called abaca from the stalk of the banana plant."

She was an animated woman, her hair in charming disarray, somewhat curly brown with an undertone of gold. She had fine lips and small hands that fluttered around the sculpture. "When abaca is damp, it's very malleable. As it dries it has a mind of its own." She laughed and went on, "I love working with paper. It's so archival—lasts forever and has so many uses."

Betty circled the piece, so taken she nearly forgot her mission. "Remarkable. The dress is so lifelike. It makes me think of Degas's dancers."

The artist came close to talk with her. "Does it? I can see the similarity."

"You live in Chicago?" Betty asked, wondering what she wanted to know anyway about the Graveswell connection. *What good will it do me to know this artist is related to that Chicago bank woman?*

The artist smiled and described her home in the city. Then they stood together silently, looking at the floating dress.

Betty felt the air humming with possibilities.

"The truth will set you free" came to her mind, a passage from John 8:32 she had quoted occasionally in her lifetime and lately to Eleanor who added President Garfield's quip, "But first it will make you miserable."

Of course, the woman's name may be a coincidence, Betty concluded, then resolved to take Jesus' advice, no matter the consequences. "Graveswell," she said offhandedly. "That's an unusual name."

"It's not the kind of name you want to marry into, but my mother did anyway." The woman laughed shaking her curls. "And I took it back after my divorce. Juliette Graveswell. Kind of Shakespearean, isn't it?" She held out her hand, which Betty took after a second's delay.

"Your parents must be very proud of your success." Betty threw out a test line. The artist looked to be in her midforties.

"My mother says I should paint portraits. There's money in that." She laughed again. "Then I could support her in her old age, but she's kidding. She'll never retire. She loves lording it over her staff at a bank."

Though her legs were trembling, Betty steeled herself and turned to another sculpture, feeling as coy as Ed on a fishing expedition.

"Yes, we all want our children to be successful." This must be the daughter in the photo of two children and their father that she had seen on Irene Graveswell's desk. *Yes, children sired by Mr. Graveswell.* Betty felt buoyant.

"My older sister and brother have already made the family proud as attorneys. So that gives me a free pass for art." The artist spun on her toes with her arm out as if presenting her art pieces. "Now don't let my chatter stop your tour of the room." She smiled briefly, her eyebrow lifting almost seductively. Betty saw it—the quirky smile, the blue eyes, sad eyes, Charlie had called them.

So, this woman is a third child, a daughter that came later! Betty made a quick review of the timeline Irene Graveswell had outlined—her unfortunate marriage, fears of poverty in the face of her husband's drinking, his death by an "L" train, the strain of widowhood, and so forth. For Betty, the whole scene of her retrieval of Charlie's safe deposit box was still vivid.

Scattered around were scenes showing Juliette Graveswell's skill in portraiture, sketches whose few strokes caught a face or body perfectly, so perfectly Betty found her husband immediately in a café scene reading his paper, head tipped in a familiar way.

Freedom was not Betty's immediate sensation. Freedom would feel like a weight lifted, a worry dispelled, a door opening. Instead, a weight fell in her stomach right on the avocado toast, which rolled itself into a lump. Her suspicions were confirmed—Charlie had indeed *helped* a pretty woman in more ways than just funding an insurance policy, as Irene Graveswell had claimed. And she had *helped* him with something Betty failed to do—produce a second child for him, yes, a sister for Sharon. This realization upset the avocado toast conclusively, and Betty rushed to the ladies' room where she locked herself in the largest stall and had a good cry, but not a long one since she had to sprint to Macy's where Eleanor was waiting by the fountain.

"I can tell by your face, it's President Garfield, dear." Eleanor handed Betty a flowered hankie. "Now, now, how bad is it?"

The two friends sat on the wide edge of the pool. The escalators zigzagged above their perch as Betty declared her certainty that Charlie had fathered the artist, Juliette Graveswell.

"Is she older or younger than your daughter?"

"Younger, I'd say by five years or so. I just can't believe he knew about her though. Charlie wasn't the kind of man who would—well—abandon a pregnant woman."

"It's possible Irene didn't tell him. He was a married man after all. Maybe she didn't want to play second fiddle to you, a wife. Too degrading."

"She had her other two children to keep out of a scandal, I suppose." Betty stood, signaling it was time to trudge out of the store toward Wabash Avenue.

"You didn't tell this Juliette your suspicions?"

"No! What good would come of that?"

"Maybe you owe her and Sharon—"

"Sharon is the last person who should know about this. She idolized her father. I won't spoil that."

Betty stepped out to cross under the "L" tracks almost before the walk signal, Eleanor clattering along with her cane shouting sentences drowned out by a train so that only "half-sisters" floated to Betty like the pigeon feathers swept up by the traffic.

15

A Phantom at the Opera

*O*nce back at the condo, Eleanor moved into high gear as fairy godmother because Betty had accepted a last-minute invitation to the opera that night from handsome Emery Fielding. Though Eleanor had also liked him, she had not responded to his blue card. In fact, Eleanor had responded to none of her potential suitors despite Betty's urging. Emery apologized for not including dinner—it was a family birthday. He suggested he meet Betty in the lobby of the condo and his car would take them to the Lyric. Betty understood some people were crazy about opera, and she wanted to find out for herself whether it was wonderful or wacky. She hoped Eleanor could prepare her sufficiently for this intimidating date.

"The opera is *Das Rheingold* by Wagner," she informed her friend.

"Ah, Hitler's favorite composer."

Betty stopped her survey of her closet. "Oh. I didn't know. Maybe I'd prefer to skip it." She was always unsure of the protocol related to Eleanor's being Jewish.

"Knowledge is power, dear. If *Das Rheingold* makes you think of the Third Reich, switch to Italian and French operas. Personally, I don't care for any opera. The plots are just too silly. We'd better google the story before you go."

"Yes, the only Rheingold I know comes in a tall glass." Betty mimicked a long swallow before they consulted the computer.

The opera is part of a trilogy referred to as the Ring Cycle, they learned. The two women read on about the theft of the river gold due to the chattiness of the river maidens, who tell the ugly Alberich that whoever steals the gold and makes it into a ring will have power over the whole world but must renounce love.

"That's quite a price to pay for power," Betty said.

"But a temptation for some, of course."

Eleanor scrolled on. This is only the beginning of the troubles, they read, as the goddess of marriage, Fricka, discovers that Wotan, her husband and lord of the gods, has promised her dear sister Freia, goddess of youth, to giants Fasolt and Fafner in return for building a fortress.

"These people are quite awful. How could the music be lovely?" Betty's opera prejudice began to solidify.

"But look at the next part. They promise all the gold to the giants in exchange for Freia. Good show for sisters!" Eleanor said, glancing at Betty with raised eyebrow. They kept reading, intrigued now.

"But the giants take her anyway, not wanting to relinquish love. And look, the gods age suddenly because they no longer have Freia's apples of youth," Betty summarized.

"Obviously, they didn't have Retin-A."

The women find there's resolution after many complications involving classic story elements: Erda, goddess of earth, warns Wotan that possession of the cursed ring will bring the death of the gods. He gives the ring to the giants and Feia reappears though Fafner clubs Fasolt to death in a quarrel over the ring. Finally, the air is cleared by thunder, lightning, and a rainbow. The Rhine maidens say tartly that the glory of the gods is merely an illusion.

"You should be ready to make scintillating comments now, Betty. 'How lovely the maidens, how fearsome the giants, how hootie the singing!'" Eleanor blasted a few operatic notes holding up her breasts.

"Eleanor!"

"They all have big chests, believe me. By the way, did Mr. Emery say where you're sitting?"

"Dress circle, I believe. What do I wear for that?"

"Very classy! Something with glitz but tasteful. Here, wear these beads with your pink sweater and skirt." She handed over a three-tiered pink crystal necklace on fine gold chains and a glittering evening bag.

"My goodness, suppose I lose these stones?"

"If someone yanks these off your neck, losing them will be the last thing we worry about." Eleanor fussed that Betty didn't have an evening coat, but added a gold embroidered Mexican shawl to her spring jacket as she left.

"Good luck, dear. Enjoy."

Betty waited, pacing in the lobby. Going out with Ed Conley had been easy. But opera! She might just be out of her element on this excursion.

Emery handed her out of the Lincoln at the Lyric Opera. Betty was unsure whether they had traveled in a hired car or family vehicle. She wondered if he had remembered exactly who she was from their first short chat in the auto since he seemed surprised when she said she was from Indiana. Their pleasantries during speed dating about big city and town life must have slipped his mind. There was little time for more conversation as they stepped into the impressive lobby. They turned over their wraps at the coat check and were jostled by many other well-dressed couples. Betty tried to take in the Art Nouveau interior without too much gawking like a first-timer. It was lovely and grand, bathed in a golden glow from the handsome lamps. Eleanor's crystals sparkled as they strolled through the chatter about the gala last week, the Phoenix opera last winter, and so forth. Betty was about to ask Emery whether he had seen other Wagner operas when he dropped her arm suddenly.

"Oh, there they are." He waved across the room. "My daughters and their husbands. And my two sisters are with them."

"How nice to meet them all," Betty said with pretended enthusiasm. These people would be a distraction from the opera requiring her to remember names and make small talk.

The couples approached, but his daughters paused to exchange words, heads together before greeting their father.

"Dad, introduce us to your friend. We heard you met at a speed dating event? How funny." The taller woman put her arm around her father.

"Betty, this is my daughter Ryan. She's a partner at Finest, Luzano, and Jones, and this is her husband Chris. And this is my daughter Dr. Graylyn with husband Pat."

They shook hands with Betty as Emery announced she was from Indiana.

"And what brings you to Chicago? Family?" the tall daughter asked.

"Visiting a friend. Actually, my daughter lives in Elkhart where she—"

"Ah, so just visiting. How nice for you." Ryan seemed to speak for everyone. The other daughter admired Betty's crystals, but it didn't feel like a compliment. Next Emery swept his arm toward his sisters, but Betty didn't quite hear their names in the din though she caught that one was his twin, a rather sour-looking lady. The other appeared much older than he and used a walker.

It was a relief to take their seats where Betty needed only to talk with her seatmates, Emery or the sister next to her. The other names had swum together, names that gave no hint as to who should wear them. Betty fell into a panic thinking how at intermission she would have to address the daughters and spouses again. For now she was glad that the oldest sister was next to her. This lady began a recital of her poor health until Emery said, rather unkindly Betty thought, "Betty is not interested in your ailments. Enough."

Betty, however, offered a few sympathetic words about the lady's colitis just as the overture began. Soon the curtain rose to the astounding sight of the Rhine maidens who swam and sang in diaphanous water so convincing Betty expected to get wet. As the scenes went on, Alberich was satisfyingly greedy and horrible; Wotan, kingly if stout; Fricka, regal with a powerful voice; and Freia, younger and quite lovely. As the solos and duets soared over the orchestra, Betty completely forgot about Emery and his family of gender-free names. She sat forward in her seat so as to not miss the projected translation while entranced by the music and sets. Maybe she was an opera lover!

Intermission was somewhat of an inquisition when she joined Emery's sisters in a trip to the ladies' room. They ferreted out information about her marital status, living situation, daughter's marital status, and daughter's husband's employment. Betty felt they gave her an exam, as well as let her know of their brother's delicate emotional state due to the loss of his wife and also of his unreliability in all matters financial. Betty surmised Emery's daughters had conveyed already that they regarded their father's invitation to Betty as merely a kindness for an acquaintance. Poor Emery surrounded by so many female guardians was unrecognizable as the witty man she had met at speed dating.

"It didn't matter, really, Eleanor," Betty told her friend during the late-night rehash about how she was made to understand that Emery was unavailable to her. She went on, "I discovered opera though. You have to give it a chance again."

Finally, after praises that reached what Eleanor said were operatic proportions, she agreed to give the art form another try, as long as it was a French comedy.

16

Epiphanies All Around

These days Vince was in a tight spot. His mother hounded him about the Lauerbachs' kitchen upgrade—Didn't he recall their last family meeting about the need to get the bottom line up? He had flinched. Yes, he would get right on... uh, get right back to Mrs. Lauerbach.

Then Lila called the company office and next Sharon's Desserts asking about a schedule for the construction. Sharon was sympathetic about his lack of enthusiasm for dealing with the Lauerbachs, though for a different reason than his at first. Finally, he told her about the incident.

"Are you serious?"

"I wouldn't make it up."

"I've heard this about her before, related to her plumber."

"Russ Ruggie?" His ego fell. Plumber's butt was Ruggie's most attractive feature.

"No, I think it was that young guy, his assistant." *Okay, that was better.* The guy was only about twenty-five with abs and curly hair. "You heard that where?"

"You'd be surprised what women tell in the beauty salon."

They were having coffee in Sharon's Desserts, which was empty after the morning rush for cinnamon rolls. Sharon handed him a cupcake that had come out a little flat. "I want to talk about Livy, Vince."

The change in topic was a relief and maybe an insult. His wife should show some worry about another woman finding him attractive, he felt. And she hadn't helped him resolve the business problem it involved.

"What am I doing with her?" Sharon said, mirroring Vince's thoughts except with a different female.

"Looks like she's settling in here."

"I know. She's nice enough, though spacey and unrealistic. But I just can't help but feel it's wrong for her to be here."

"Wrong? She likes you a lot."

"You think?" Sharon thought about how just today she had reminded her twice about cleanup being essential.

"Absolutely. She hangs on your every word."

"I do like her in spite of, well, Daddy's affair. But I feel so disloyal to Mother who never did the slightest wrong thing in her life."

Working side-by-side and listening to Livy's chatter about her friends, her classes, and her boyfriend was a troubling pleasure. Sharon sighed. "This guilt makes me feel like sometimes I just want to send her home and forget the whole thing." She rested her forehead in her hands. "Where is this leading? What is the possible happy ending?" She looked at her husband.

That, Vince wasn't able to say.

So quickly had they gotten used to having Livy in the house too that it was obvious she was filling a void for them. They watched her face light up over certain texts and tried to lift her spirits if none came. They got used to the washing machine running at odd hours and her making them a supper tray if they worked late. She had settled into the bedroom reserved for Betty's visits because it turned out she had no need to return to Chicago since she wasn't enrolled for the next college term. Instead she was supposed to be on an internship or observation in her field of interest. She explained that she had entered college in the fall to study fabric design (as encouraged by her mother), had changed her course of study by January to interior design (because it's more marketable), and was now considering changing to retail management (her father's choice for practicality).

One afternoon as the three of them lingered at the shop at closing time, Livy jumped up. "It's so obvious!" She twirled around the shop like the ingénue in a musical comedy. "I love this! I love this!" she sang, spreading out her arms. "Someday I want to be a great dessert chef like you." She hugged Sharon and spun again.

"Olivia's wedding cakes! Olivia's opulent octagonal oatmeal opus. Or no," now speaking seductively, "Livy's Little Lair of Lusciousness." Sharon and Vince laughed.

Then grabbing a rolling pin Livy posed as anchorwoman. "Headline news: Master pastry chef Olivia Riley prepared her signature cherries jubilee at the White House state dinner for the French president."

Then her shoulders slumped. "Riley is kind of a common name though. Do you think Graveswell would be sort of a downer name for a chef? I know, Olivia D'Angelo would be so much better, don't you think so, Uncle Vince?"

She dropped into a chair between Sharon and Vince, smiling more fully than they had seen since her arrival. Throwing caution to the wind, Sharon suggested she stay for the term, working at the shop to see if her culinary interest held. Livy assured Sharon that she could stay, that her mother was happy she was visiting an Indiana friend and not her boyfriend.

"She hates that he's in a band. A loser just like my dad, she says. So, this arrangement makes her happy. And I guess it might even if she knew the whole story. She's kind of spacey though."

Not being parents themselves, Sharon and Vince couldn't share in the delicacies of this analysis. Though they were uncomfortable about the perfidy involved, Sharon met this dilemma by simply hiding her curiosity about the woman dismissed as *spacey* who was her half-sister and also putting off any serious talk with Betty.

Every conversation with her mother was circumspect. No, she didn't need Betty to help with spring rush quite yet. "Everything is going just fine here, thank you," she told her mother. "You can stay on with Eleanor."

"Oh, all right, then, dear. That's fine, goodbye."

Sharon was puzzled that her mother gave up quickly— almost with relief—on the idea of returning to Elkhart anytime soon. *Was this dating thing getting out of hand in the city?* Sharon forbade herself from thinking about her mother hooking up, or whatever it might be called for seniors. She was astonished when Betty mentioned winning a trip to New York with one guy. Though it seemed very out of character for her mother to actually go, it would keep her busy for even longer. Maybe a ripening social life would soften the letdown of learning about Livy, for it would take putting the girl out on the street to prevent an eventual meeting with accompanying revelations or elaborate lies.

17

The Roving Eye

*B*ecause she needed shop coverage in addition to Livy, who was making six dozen cupcakes, Sharon, with reluctance, asked Mary.

"I'll be gone about two hours. Thanks so much for coming to help."

Sharon hugged her mother-in-law, noting a hint of floral musk. The expensive scent was something else new since Manny's death. In fact, Mary was quite changed, now that Sharon took a look at her. Today she wore narrow black pants, a black sweater, a gold rope around her neck, and, yes, caramel-colored, heeled boots. *Where was the woman going?* Perhaps these days Mary would feel helping in the shop was beneath her.

Livy came out from the back, a dab of pink frosting on her pink hair. Sharon moved into the difficult introduction.

"This is Mrs. D'Angelo, Vince's mother, Livy. And Mary, this is Olivia."

"Pleased to meet you, Mrs. D'Angelo." Livy held out a sticky hand.

"Olivia who?" Mary held her offered hand at length.

"Riley, ma'am."

"Yes, she's here learning about being a dessert chef and running a shop." Sharon gathered cake boxes for the party she was setting up. She looked up to see Mary appraise Livy. *Oh God,* she thought, trying not to glance at her father's photo.

"I can see that she's a relative of yours," Mary said as Sharon hustled Livy out the door with some trash.

"She's from Chicago."

"I didn't know you have family in Illinois."

"Well, one never knows," Sharon said, wondering how long she could keep up this cat-and-mouse game.

With a waft of perfume, Mary whisked to the shelf with Charlie's photo.

"How true. Then you find out." Mary studied the photo. "Is she a niece?"

The game was up. Sharon nodded her head and found herself embracing Mary who patted her back as she wept into the gold rope necklace. "Is it that obvious?" She daubed at Mary's sweater and sniffed.

"It's no surprise to me. Long time ago I opened your back door to drop off a pie for your mother. Your father, he was on your hall phone with a woman, all lovey-dovey. Now we see the result."

Sharon pictured the old-fashioned telephone stand in the hall by the closet. She used to pull the phone in there for private conversations. Apparently her father wasn't as smart.

"How could he have done that to Mother, to us? I'm afraid I hate him now." Sharon twisted the edge of her jacket.

Mary took her fingers and massaged them. "No, no. Don't feel that way. Some men wander once in a while. Wives expected it—the roving eye."

"But it's terrible what he did. I don't want Mother to find out."

"Good luck with that one." Mary took out a compact from her purse to rearrange her necklace. "Well, I certainly won't tell her." Sharon gave a drier hug to her mother-in-law who went on, "By the way, tell Vince that Lila Lauerbach called again today. He needs to get on with the next step in her remodel."

"I think he said he didn't have time for the project at all," Sharon said, turning away to exchange the cherry chip cupcakes with the fudge dream in the display case. She felt Mary's hand on her shoulder.

"Sharon, for Vincenzo you're the sun, moon, and stars." Sharon thought she caught an implication of incredulity. "Don't worry. Let him work on the lady's kitchen. No roving eye on my handsome boy." Mary looked out the window toward their business, then added, "Not like his father."

"Oh no! So sorry. I didn't know that Mr. D'Angelo—" Sharon felt more tears coming.

"Never mind. A good wife used to overlook. Like Mrs. Clinton." Sharon thought she saw a warning sent her way before Mary tied on one of the paisley aprons.

"Now, what is it we—your niece with the lovely name and me—should do while you're out?" Mary surveyed the display case. "How about if I show Olivia how to make *torta caprese*?" She pronounced it with a flourish. "That would go good with the coffee here. And look so special. So much better than what they call flourless chocolate cake like you have there." She pointed.

Sharon sighed, never sure which feeling related to Mary was stronger, irritation or amusement. This time, their conversation left much to mull over. Apparently, the woman knew how to keep a secret. That was for sure.

18

No Way to Wiggle Out

In the Lake Shore Drive condo, Betty and Eleanor were in a mild argument. Eleanor was insisting they get pedicures to break up the long, cloudy afternoon.

"It's called a pedi for short, Betty."

"I can't imagine showing my feet to anyone."

"Don't you sometimes go to a lake in the summer?"

"That's different. Your feet are way down there in water. Now, in summer I might have sandals on, so there'd be a point to a pedi." She tried out the jargon, but it came out as a belittlement.

"A nice nail trim is always refreshing, Betty. Think of it as medical."

"In that case I'd go to a podiatrist. They look at feet all day."

"The nail artists look at feet all day and charge a lot less, believe me. Now I'm going to call for appointments. Move over." Eleanor reached for the phone on the table by Betty.

"Just make one for yourself." Betty sat solidly still.

"Well, aren't you considering going to New York with Ed? You'll need pretty toes for that. This can be just a dry run. Please?" Eleanor launched into a negotiation with someone at Vegas Nails ordering side-by-side pedis.

"Linh and Lan have openings in a half an hour."

"I'd better take a bath first."

"For heaven's sake, Betty, you're just going to take your socks off." Eleanor got their jackets and tossed Betty hers.

As they took the elevator to the street and headed to Vegas Nails a block away, Eleanor gave further instructions about color choice, sparkle versus sheen, water temperature, massage chair adjustments, and tipping until Betty tried to turn around.

"I just don't like the unknown."

"You won't feel like Alice in Wonderland with me there. Haven't you had your fingernails done? Every woman of a certain age I know does that."

"Of course. For Sharon's wedding and our fiftieth party."

"And that was how long ago?"

"Oh, stop smirking. Besides, at home at the NuLook I never saw a pedicure given. A pedi." By one styling chair there was that tank that looked like an old-fashioned ringer mop bucket, Betty recalled, but she never saw any feet in it.

"Well, a nice pedi can change your life. You'll see." Eleanor yanked open the door just missing chopping off Betty's toes. The chemical odors of beauty embraced them immediately.

"Hello mama, hello mama!" An Asian woman helped them take off their jackets as Betty took in that the greeting was directed toward them. "Pick your colors. Then we're ready." The woman hung up their things and pointed to the nail polish display.

Following Eleanor's lead, Betty stepped to the rack and was transfixed by the choices. Not wanting to look indecisive, she quickly reached toward a very pale pink, certainly tasteful. Eleanor snatched it and put it back.

"Betty, this is costing thirty-five dollars. Choose something fun." She rummaged through the bottles. "Look, I'm going to have Purple Passion Flower."

"Something for spring, mama?" The proprietress intervened holding out a nauseous bright pink with a silver sheen.

"Not that one, but thank you," Betty said thinking it would look as if she had dipped her toes in diarrhea medicine. "I'll choose one myself." Her hand hovered here and there over the racks.

"Take your time, mama. It's okay." The proprietress settled behind her desk again.

From Apple Blush to Zodiac Green, Betty wondered if there was some sort of choice protocol by foot type, cost, or age. She couldn't remember what all Eleanor had said before, but if lurid purple was all right for Eleanor, then she could choose her favorite color—turquoise. Hawaiian Moonlight with its silver glitter seduced her, no matter if blue toes were unnatural except in frostbite or death.

"Here. How about this one?" Betty held it out for Eleanor's approval and saw that Linh and Lan were standing next to deep tubs. Eleanor led the way and was helped into a large chair. Her cane was laid on the floor and her shoes removed gently.

"Just sit down, Betty, and let her take off your shoes. Don't look so pained. You're having fun," Eleanor said settling back in the lounge chair.

Betty complied while Linh slipped off her sneakers, dumped some powder that effervesced in the tub, and gently lifted her feet into the water.

"Oh, it's like stepping into soup."

"Too hot?" Her pedicurist looked alarmed.

"Oh no. Just a surprise." Betty tittered when milky pink fizz covered her feet to the calves and sent off a flowery scent.

"It's okay?"

"Yes, okay." The girl—as that's what the slim Linh seemed to be—gently pressed Betty back in the chair and fiddled with the buttons on a remote that she gave to Betty.

"You enjoy massage." She patted the white towel she had folded on the footrest. Betty deduced that she was to put a foot there. Then Linh guided her heel into place gently, assisting in the tricky lift of her calf. Betty peeked at her foot, hoping it was nice enough to show this delicate young woman who perhaps would shrink back and put on a mask or something. Indeed, were she and Eleanor taking advantage of these Vietnamese newcomers, presenting their feet to those lowly enough to be required to tend to them? On the other hand, foot washing had become an Eastertime ritual at her church where to wash another's feet was to show Christ-like humility. Shouldn't she be washing this lovely woman's feet? Such thoughts were derailed by a *hr-urr* in her chair as it came to life, deconstructing into mechanics that rolled and tumbled, working their way along her back like busy elves.

"My goodness!" Betty sat forward. Then hearing Eleanor sigh in her chair, Betty gingerly leaned back and understood that the remote controlled the massage. She dialed a lower number. With a gurgle, the chair obeyed, delivering gentle waves that were amazing, Betty had to admit.

She took a critical look at the foot on the towel. Her shoe size hadn't changed in all these years and her ankles remained trim, a wonder really. She lifted the foot in the water to appraise the other ankle—both very nice, unlike the meaty ankles of several friends. But it was wrong, and possibly bad karma, to feel superior over her own heart's efficiency. She closed her eyes for a moment of contrition. However, Charlie's voice, more unreachable to her as the years piled up, reinvigorated her prideful thoughts.

"Yours are Hollywood gams, doll." His voice was so perfectly clear she looked around. *Had his spirit come to a nail salon?*

He had liked legs and hers in particular. She snuggled into her massage chair to daydream. Early in their marriage how he had liked to wrap his fingers around an ankle while she giggled and protested, a game evolving into a quiet bedtime routine until their last shared night.

"Bring your Hollywood gams here, madam!" he always called to her. She would find her side of the bed warm with the covers turned back invitingly.

"I said, 'What was she like?'" Eleanor shook Betty's arm.

"Who?" Surely Eleanor wasn't referring to Linh.

"The artist. Juliette Graveswell." The name chased away Betty's vision of the marriage bed.

"Oh, she seemed nice."

"Everyone seems *nice* to you, Betty. What was she like?"

"I'm not sure that I could really say." Betty realized the pedi was intended to make this chat about Juliette inescapable. She could hardly jump out of the footbath and stalk out.

"Come off it, Betty. Did Juliette look like your husband?" Eleanor punctuated her question by pounding Betty's arm gently. "Or your daughter, even?"

"It's not just a soap opera, Eleanor." Though in truth that was the best analogy Betty could think of for this shocking turn in her ordinary life. But Eleanor was genuinely curious, and so far Betty had evaded her friend's questions, so she relented.

"Actually, the woman looked quite a bit like her, uh, her father through the eyes. Yes, she did look like my Charlie."

"You found out for certain?"

"Indirectly, yes. She said her mother works at First Capital Bank. So I don't think it could be just a coincidence in last names."

"You're right, I guess. I'm sorry. Really." She took Betty's hand across the gap in their seats. They sat for a few minutes while their chairs murmured in sympathy. Betty watched as her foot tenderly scrubbed by Linh sent delicious messages to her brain.

The arrival of a new client enlivened the salon. The newcomer rushed to another woman already waiting who was fortyish, the new arrival a little older. They embraced, chose colors, and settled in side-by-side for manicures. Their conversation floated over to Betty who was in a daze as Linh began a leg massage so lovely Betty tried to recall if even sex had felt this great.

"Did you see Dad for his seventieth?" the older woman said.

"God, yes. I went to the party my mother threw. Believe me, lucky you for being away."

"The food?"

"Vegan. I don't think you would have known anyone there. So you escaped introducing yourself as first daughter, yadda, yadda, yadda." She made a rolling gesture with her finger.

"Glad I had to miss it. I'll take Dad to lunch next weekend."

"Not on Sunday, though. The matinee tickets, remember?"

"Sure, we'll be there. Ray can't wait to spill the beans about his promotion. Don't say you already heard."

The women chatted on, got out phones to show photos, sent texts, and laughed that they chose the same polish color. They were sisters, Betty deduced, half-sisters, but the warmth between them was obvious.

"You like color?" Her own artist had applied Hawaiian Moonlight to one toe.

Betty leaned slightly for a good look. "It's beautiful." An adjective that wasn't much of an exaggeration. Her naked toes glowed pink and felt deliciously smooth and tingly. The turquoise polish would be the final touch, a fountain of youth. Eleanor interrupted her communion with her feet.

"Now, Betty, while we're here we should hash over what you should do about artist Graveswell."

"It seems to me best that sleeping dogs—" Her aphorism was cut off by the laughter of the sisters, who sat with their hands under the manicure dryer but were trying to send texts.

"What about if the *sleeping dogs* might like each other?" Eleanor followed Betty's glance to the women.

"What do you mean?"

"Your silence about your husband's affair is denying Sharon knowing her half-sister."

How true. Here was the sister Sharon had always wanted as a child. And here, Betty's thoughts jerked ahead, was someone to fill her own place, for she would leave Sharon at some point. But admitting immediately that Eleanor was right was just too much.

"I'll think about it, Eleanor, and that's that. Now let me enjoy the rest of my pedi." She dialed her chair massage up a notch.

Once back at the condo, Betty closed the bedroom door, sat on her bed, and took off her shoes and socks. Her feet looked well tended, and the turquoise polish event had turned out to be pampering she was anxious to describe for Sharon. It wasn't closing time yet at the dessert shop, but perhaps Sharon would welcome a little break. She dialed the shop and the phone was answered immediately by a woman with a slight accent.

"Sharon's Desserts. Can I help you?"

Oh, it was Vince's mother helping out again. "How are you, Mary? I wonder if I may speak with my daughter." Betty bristled, picturing Mary in a sloppy housedress minding the cute shop. *What kind of mother am I, gallivanting around getting pedis when my daughter needs help?* Betty got out her pocket calendar.

"We're doing good," Mary said. "How do you like city living?"

"It's certainly more fast-paced, but I'm thinking of coming back to Indiana for a spell." Betty flipped a calendar page. Yes, she could cancel an upcoming date and her hair appointment and go to Indiana day after tomorrow by bus or train.

"Very dull here. You will like the city better."

How much time was that woman spending at the shop? Betty aimed to find out. "Sharon must be busy these days?"

"Yes, yes. She is taking orders for special Mother's Day baskets."

"I hadn't heard about those." Betty felt she had just sounded whiny.

"We fill a basket with muffins, tea, and napkins with even mother's name, if desired."

Betty caught *we* more than the basket details. Mary was much more involved than necessary at Sharon's Desserts. She should be back at D'Angelo and Sons minding the phone there. Betty could hear someone else saying "I'm back." No doubt a store regular. Then Mary added, "You want to leave a message?"

"No, thanks. I'll just call my daughter later."

"I'll tell her. Bye." It seemed to Betty that Mary was very anxious to get off the phone.

19

What They Say in New York . . .

The sisters in the salon came back to Betty as she sat in her room in the evening jotting a few impressions in her daybook. Perhaps her reticence about the Graveswells was wrong. But how could she know for certain? She couldn't picture talking it over with the minister of her church and probably couldn't afford a fancy counselor. She made a list of pros and cons for telling Sharon about her father's liaison. The sides seemed about equal, with one exception.

Pro—*Honesty was usually the best policy. (Sharon should know family history.)*

Con—*Don't tell something hurtful in the name of honesty. (Didn't Charlie's escapade fall in this category?)*

Pro—*Sharon might want to meet these people.*

Con—*They might not want to meet Sharon. (From their silence this seemed to be the case.)*

Pro—*Sharon might really like the Graveswells.*

Con—*Sharon might really like the Graveswells.*

Betty put down her pen. *How awful of me to feel that way,* she scolded herself. Perhaps she needed to see her minister after all.

Her list making was interrupted by her phone, Sharon's ringtone.

"Hi, dear. Thanks for calling."

"Mary said you called earlier." Sharon couldn't guess yet the nature of this communication since her mother had left no message.

"Yes, I just wondered how things are going at the shop and at home."

Had her mother gotten wind of Livy? She looked at the girl busily thumbing out texts on her phone. Well, surely her mother didn't text.

"We're very busy—Vince and I. He's going to do over a kitchen, though I'm not too thrilled with the job. The woman is positively throwing herself at him." She described Lila's behavior at the catered party.

"You've nothing to worry about, Sharon. Vince is solid as a church."

Was this the same misplaced faith her mother had years ago about her own husband? Sharon pushed away the thought.

Betty changed the subject. "Mary," emphasis on the name, "said you are doing baskets for Mother's Day."

This seemed like a safe topic and Sharon warmed to telling Betty all about the number of orders piling up on this unique seasonal item. It felt so good to boast to her mother about the success story. She relaxed for the first time that evening, chatting while watching Vince get lessons in texting from Livy. It had taken her niece only a few days to persuade Mr. Phoneless to get a smartphone.

"Maybe you need an extra hand this month, dear?"

Sharon heard her mother's gentle voice rattle on. "I'm looking at my calendar and I could be there day after tomorrow. Then you wouldn't have to rely on Mary." Sharon tuned back in on the word "tomorrow," her relaxed attitude fleeing.

"Mother, that's not necessary." She could picture Betty already throwing things in a suitcase. "You probably already have engagements planned. We're—I'm doing fine on the baskets."

"I can easily change things. It's no problem and I want to help you."

"Right now it helps me to know you are having fun with dating in Chicago." This was a lie but it was the strongest discouragement she could think of.

"My life isn't about fun, Sharon. It's about being of use. Why should you have to rely on Vince's mother when you have your own mother available?"

So, this threatened return is about Mary, not about Livy. Granted, Mary was second best, but this was no time to have her mother arrive, and she couldn't very well send Livy away now that they were knee-deep in complex orders, with more every day. Her fingers gripping the phone began to tingle.

"Believe me, Mom, I miss you, but this is just not a good time to have you here. Vince is painting your room, as a surprise for your Mother's Day visit." That should cap it off, though not a surprise Vince had time for these days.

Her mother was silent a moment. "I see I might be in the way." Then continuing in a theatrically cheerful voice, she added, "I'll just go ahead then and take the trip to NYC."

"New York?"

"Yes, remember that I won a trip with Ed Conley. He's been asking me about when we're going."

"So soon? Where are you staying?"

"Somewhere very posh, Ed said. He seems to know about these things."

"But it's important you know where, Mother. Now you let me know the name and I'll check it out and—"

Sharon stopped midsentence. Here was the answer right in front of her face. If her mother had a boyfriend, no, a companion, *boyfriend* with its unthinkable associations wasn't right, it just might soften the blow of the Graveswell relationship when it came.

"Of course I'll email you the dates and hotel, dear. I suppose we'll take some tours too."

"Yes, Mom, do have a good time. Just think, you'll see the Statue of Liberty and the Empire State Building." She named sights sure to lock in her mother's snap decision.

"Yes, maybe I'll find out why they call it the Big Apple."

"For sure. And bring us souvenirs." Sharon stumbled on *us* again, adding, "I'm sure Vince would like an NYC doodad for his dashboard."

This phrase caught his attention, and he labored over his keypad sending a text of jumbled letters to her phone.

Betty and Sharon signed off with the usual "love yous."

Vince said, "You're going to have to tell her sometime, Sharon. Didn't you just say she's here for Mother's Day?"

"I have to go home?" Livy jumped up. "I want to be here for the basket deliveries."

"You should be with your own mother on Mother's Day," Sharon said.

"We don't celebrate it because Mom says it's a commercial holiday. And it contributes to the subjugation of women through the subversive means of honoring motherhood."

"Barefoot and pregnant in the kitchen, yes." Vince adjusted the lounge chair backwards and crossed his hands over his stomach. "Bring me a beer, women."

He heard his name shouted twice, one preceded by uncle and followed by a flying pillow. He ducked.

"Guess, that means I get my own beer."

"But you should be with your mother, nevertheless." Sharon felt Mother's Day bearing down like an express train, with not just the baskets to deliver but the extra baggage of Betty and the annual elaborate dinner with all the D'Angelos.

"Mom would say I'm taken in by crass commercialism, unless I bought art as a Mother's Day gift, of course. That would be all right with her. I told you she was weird." Livy shrugged.

The subject was closed for Livy, but for Sharon somewhat open. She was always irked by Mother's Day, even this year when it was bringing her a bounty of business. The commercials struck her as sanctimonious, from the adorable kids with goofy dads, to grandmothers flanked by grandkids, to diamond jewelry gifts. And then these scenes were played out in real time at Vince's mother's house where she and her own mother sat on the sidelines while Mary was honored by the large D'Angelo family. Perhaps Livy's mother was on to something, was someone with whom she shared a sensibility. Her curiosity to meet this woman began to turn from a hard knot into a bud.

Livy patted the couch inviting Sharon to sit.

"Aunt Sharon, look at this. I googled how to be a celebrity chef. There are all kinds of tips here for you."

"I'm not hoping to be a celebrity, just make it through the first cut."

"Okay, listen to this. It says you need to like to talk about yourself."

"Negative on that one," said Vince. Sharon tended to be circumspect on personal topics.

"It doesn't mean like a big ego. It means telling stories about food and cooking in your life. So, how about some stories, Aunt Sharon? When did you make your first dessert?" Livy folded her arms and leaned back.

"I was a champion at s'mores. I pioneered the peanut butter and jelly giant s'more at scout camp." Sharon went on at length about the exploding marshmallow fluff jar, rambler's foil-wrapped stew, and her cooking badge. Her animation surprised Vince and kept Livy from glancing at her phone.

In the condo the next day, Betty sought out Eleanor to explain her intention of taking the New York trip.

"That will let you wiggle out of talking with Sharon about the artist."

"You must be psychic." Betty sighed.

Eleanor was laying out several cheeses and crackers along with a pot of tea, their usual lunch if at home.

"I'm just not sure what to do." Betty flapped a page of the *Tribune*.

"These obituaries remind me I won't be around forever. Sharon has Vince and his family but no one close from her father's family or mine. She has nothing in common with my sister's son and his wife in Texas. My other sisters are gone now and never married. So she'd be alone without Vince, except for his brother."

"You said the artist Juliette seemed nice. And she lives here." Eleanor set a slice of blue cheese on a water cracker. Betty wrinkled her nose.

"It's very well for you to give advice, Eleanor, but look at it from my perspective."

"Which is?"

"Well, there's the money issue. Suppose Juliette wants more of Charlie's estate?"

"Didn't he leave his estate to you?"

"Yes, with Sharon as beneficiary. But couldn't his other daughter have a reasonable claim?"

"Does she have children?"

"That's another thing. Sharon doesn't, so somehow it could look as if this woman deserves more if she does have children. And furthermore she is divorced, so she might be short of money."

"And an artist to boot," added Eleanor. The women nodded over this unstable profession.

"There's something else too. She might, I don't know, lord it over Sharon, even inadvertently." Betty recalled the artist's lighthearted manner, the eye makeup, the confidence in her craft.

"You mean she's more attractive?"

"Actually, her face was careworn in spite of her makeup. Oh, this is so silly." Betty began to cry. "I haven't even told you the worst."

"What could it be?"

"Well, suppose, Juliette and that Irene, her mother, get on like peas and carrots. They're both quite glamorous and worldly. Suppose Sharon—"

"Oh, I know exactly what you mean. It's not silly at all." Eleanor put her arm around Betty. "I worry all the time that my daughter will want to spend more time with her father and aunt in Florida than with me."

"But she lives in Chicago sometimes."

"Yes, but her father understands her better than I do." Eleanor sighed.

"I guess we are a couple of—"

"Jealous bitches?"

"I was going to say worrywarts." Betty laughed, sniffing.

"Oh, but it doesn't have the satisfying ring."

Betty got out a hankie, a feminine accessory she and Eleanor were trying to revive, and dabbed at her face. "I ask myself, what would Charlie want?"

"Shouldn't it be, what do you want?"

"That question doesn't seem to get me an answer. The big picture includes him after all. What I want is for Sharon to be happy and fulfilled. What do I need to do to assure that?"

"She's middle-aged, Betty, not a kid where you're responsible for her happiness."

"I know, I know." Fresh tears fell. "I guess I want it to be my responsibility. That's mothering."

"How about this? Maybe you need to follow your instinct that Sharon should know about her sister. Then you should have faith in her to work out the details."

They contemplated this course of action while pouring more tea.

"Here's an idea." Betty set down her cup with gusto. "I'll send a note to Juliette to introduce myself. I'll let her know a time and place I will be at the Cultural Center. Then if she comes to meet me, we'll go from there."

"Brilliant! A plan that looks stalwart and lets you waffle at the same time. Here, have some of this blue cheese for more valor." Eleanor shoved the plate toward her friend.

"Not on your life." Betty took a slice of moon-yellow Edam, shoving it between two water crackers that shattered satisfyingly as she took a bite. The hankie whisked the crumbs to the carpet, and the women laughed as Eleanor took the lunch remains to the kitchen, guiding the blue cheese under Betty's nose as she passed.

Next Eleanor listened while Betty phoned Ed with the good news that she was ready to go to New York anytime. By four, he called back, saying the travel agent they were assigned had rushed the arrangements and they were to leave in two days.

"Oh goody," said Eleanor. "I get the fun of packing without the aggravation of going."

In the evening, they headed for Betty's room, dragging out two pieces of matching floral luggage from the closet. "Of course, you'll use these. Yours are much too ratty."

Argument ensued as items flew in and out of the suitcase and carry-on for the next two hours.

"Don't you have a better nightgown? Silk pajamas? Or a matching robe or fluffy mules?" They had settled on the clothes, things for day and evening wear, and were down to what Eleanor called "the essentials."

"I'm sure this nightwear will be fine." Betty folded the pale floral tricot quickly. "Sharon gave me the robe for Christmas."

"It's nice, but your nightie looks limp. We need to go shopping."

"Oh, I don't know about this whole thing." Betty sat down on the bed.

"What do you mean? You're going on a free trip to New York. Just get a nicer nightgown and don't worry." Eleanor zipped the larger bag shut. "You know what they say in New York, don't you?"

"What?"

"Fuhgeddaboudit."

Betty looked blank.

"It's Italian. Google it," Eleanor said, rolling the larger pretty bag toward the front door where it would be out of Betty's reach for unpacking in case of cold feet.

20

What's Cookin'?

*I*n Elkhart, the D'Angelo household found the audition, Mother's Day baskets, and Lauerbachs' kitchen more pressing than dwelling on the real problem at hand—how long could Livy be kept a secret? Though her niece insisted her daily calls satisfied her mother that she was staying with a friend, Sharon began to consider whether this lie didn't put her and Vince in a bad light, and here she hadn't even met this sister in person. An Internet search had yielded reviews of Juliette's art exhibits, a public radio interview, several videos, and her website. Sharon, by watching the videos covertly, now knew her sister's speech mannerisms and recognized a hair toss that was the same as Livy's. From studying photos of herself and of Juliette, she didn't think she and Juliette strongly resembled each other. People always said she favored Betty, but both sisters' coloring appeared similar to their father's. And unlike Livy whose hair was straight and thick, the sisters had their father's wavy hair. Juliette was younger. She appeared more animated and held strong opinions, making pronouncements in interviews Sharon wouldn't think of sharing. Sharon wondered if they would really have anything in common if they met in person. *Well, other than Livy.* She dreaded when Livy wouldn't be around the house and shop, even though she frequently had to correct her, or at least wanted to, sometimes so often she wondered whether Livy would pick up her backpack and just leave. Nevertheless, Livy stayed on. She rarely mentioned her mother and what she did say made Sharon guess they didn't get on well. And she had to admit guilty pride in the enthusiasm and warmth Livy had for her and Vince, even though this might only be a hiatus from her mother.

"Don't teenagers always hate their parents?" Sharon asked Vince one night. The girl's warmth might not signal a genuine familial endorsement of the D'Angelos at all.

On a Monday when the shop was closed, Sharon came back from the market to find two young men in her kitchen setting up cameras and lights.

"Livy?" Sharon said from the door.

"This is Tink and Grant. Guys, this is Mrs. D'Angelo, my Aunt Sharon." She wrapped an arm around Sharon.

They offered a "hey" and shook hands vigorously. Grant had a full beard and Tink a ponytail.

"Nice kitchen, ma'am." Tink spread the feet on a light stand on her granite counter. "Mind if I move these?" He handed Sharon potted basil and chives.

"Did I forget to tell you they're here to do some videos for you?" Livy beamed at Sharon and shoved napkins and a bag of carrots into a drawer.

"Livy! Of course you forgot to tell me." Sharon moved the carrots from the drawer to the fridge. "What are they doing? Here, put a potholder under that stand on the granite."

Livy began to unwind a blue power cord Sharon recognized as Vince's. "I knew you'd be happy to help them get camera practice for their films class, and you need practice making a flan in front of cameras. Best of all, you can use the videos for your social media channels."

"I can make flan with my eyes closed," Sharon said, and then retreated to the pantry to scold herself. *Good grief, I sound just like Mother being difficult.* Also, she didn't want to admit her online presence was quite minimal.

Livy followed her there, coiling the extra power cord into a neat nest as impressive as if Vince had done it. "Yeah, but you have to practice talking about making flan and making flan at the same time."

Grant, who looked a lot like his namesake in full beard, was threading a fine wire over her light fixture. "What's flan?"

"It's pronounced like 'blond,' not 'fan.' *Flan*," said Livy. "Haven't you ever ordered dessert in a Mexican restaurant?" Livy began to evaluate the set, making a tower of fruit on a footed dish she set on the counter. "Is that okay for camera one, Tink?"

Sharon got a lime from the fridge and set it on top of the fruit, moving the dish a bit left. "Actually, flan dates back to the ancient Romans who made the dish as a savory with eel or with honey and sugar. Their dishes spread over Europe with them and then to the Americas." Sharon began to warm to the topic before she remembered that this project had taken over her kitchen without her permission. She adjusted the fruit again.

"Count me out on eel flan," Tink said exaggerating the vowel sound.

"Aunt Sharon's going to make classic caramel flan. You'll be drooling."

As Livy moved to the center island near the stove for a sound check, the whole thing snapped into place for Sharon. Hadn't she planned this kitchen as a showplace for demonstration? Wasn't that the point of the island, the spotlights, and countertop six-burner stove? How was this different from the instruction she used to give at demo parties when she sold utensils they stored in the garage? The wish she kept in her heart stirred—*Sharon D'Angelo's Midwest Kitchen*. Articles, a cookbook, weekend cooking retreats, and cuisine travel with pastry chef Sharon D'Angelo!

"Aunt Sharon? What do you think? Should the ingredients be pre-measured?"

Sharon sprang into action with her instincts for instruction. She changed her clothes, made backup preps, and warmed up the oven. Chatter and laugher flew around the kitchen, the ages and experience of the crew melding into one creative unit.

During the first takes at Sharon's, the airport transport pulled up at Eleanor's condo.

"Oh goody for you. A stretch!" said Eleanor when an impressively long, white vehicle nosed into the no parking zone.

"Big Apple, here I come," Betty called to her friend as the driver collected her luggage and swept open the door. He took her elbow to steady her. It was much nicer than clambering into Sharon's vehicle from a step stool that made her feel conspicuously decrepit. *I should be thankful,*

Betty chided herself. *Sharon was doing what she thought best after all.*

Betty could just make out Ed on a seat way in the back wearing a tan zip jacket and his USS *Wisconsin* USN cap, which he had worn for two of the three occasions they had met. She inched her way past a credenza holding stemware and napkins, ducked under red and green parrot lights, and dropped onto a bench at an angle to Ed on the back seat.

"This is some ride," he said and helped her arrange her jacket, a lively quilted navy with a daffodil print lining that showed at the neck and cuffs.

"It's bigger than a hearse. Maybe he's going to pick up other people too." Betty tucked her yellow scarf in her navy purse with the three partitions and gold clasp, Eleanor's one concession to letting her fall back on her old fashion habits.

"You folks comfortable?" The driver slid the partition aside to talk. "I wanna treat you right. Drinks in the bar. How about music? You like Reggae?"

Horns and marimbas filled the air as the limo swayed along Outer Lake Shore Drive to find its way to an interstate ramp. Slow traffic gave Betty and Ed plenty of time to admire the driver's ingenuity in being ready for any social occasion.

"We could celebrate Mardi Gras, Christmas, or Cinco de Mayo with all the trimmings," Ed said offering Betty some maracas and a long string of purple beads.

"And there's plenty of white twinkle bell lights for a wedding." She pointed to the lights along the side windows.

"Or how about these?" Ed pulled out some men's magazines that were hiding behind some travel glossies.

"Goodness!" Betty giggled. "Maybe he's driving a bachelor party tonight." *Or maybe men read these on a ride to the airport,* she thought. This gave her passing unease and led to wondering what Ed's expectations were for their hotel stay. In fact, what about her own expectations? She pushed away the thought to collect more limo details for Eleanor later.

Their driver used an intercom to reach them. "Sure you folks don't want something to drink? There's orange juice, water, and champagne. The company ordered that. You folks celebrating a wedding anniversary?"

It did look that way, Betty supposed, though she couldn't imagine what a lifetime with Ed would have been like beyond a lot of television and fishing. And sprucing him up from time to time—*but that wasn't really fair.* He had mentioned that his wife died several years before but was gentleman enough not to talk about her on a date.

Ed answered the driver. "Actually we won this trip to New York City on our first date at a sales dinner."

"So, you're not married?"

"Just friends," Betty piped up but then worried she had hurt Ed's feelings. "Good friends." She patted his arm.

"I'm going to see New York City with a lovely lady. What could be better?" Ed caught the driver's eye in the mirror. He took his hands off the wheel for a thumbs-up.

The music switched to "New York, New York" with Liza Minnelli singing her heart out and Ed joining in. Betty forced her gaze away from the swaying parrots, determined to keep her breakfast in place. Ed pointed out some white bags discretely tucked behind the magazines, but her stomach rallied once she changed to a seat facing forward and the limo was swooping down the interstate straightaway.

Later she told Eleanor the sales company had thought of everything to stay in their good graces. After all, they were potential timeshare clients. The driver helped carry their bags inside where after a confusing few minutes printing boarding passes, they were met by airport transport. *Thank goodness not wheelchairs,* Betty thought. Old age proved a blessing at security since they could keep their shoes on but was of no help in avoiding screening. Ed's remark "So much easier than a colonoscopy" was met by stone faces from the TSA agents who waved him and then Betty through the screening column. When another agent unzipped Betty's bag, she was embarrassed when her new pink lacy gown slid out. Surely the young woman bit her tongue not to say, "At your age? Really, lady!" bringing to Betty even more clearly the hotel room ahead.

While Betty and Ed were in transit, back in Elkhart Vince stepped into an alien world when he lumbered into the kitchen for a sandwich. He had just maneuvered past Lila Lauerbach's offers of coffee, beer, or lunch, her gestures calling to mind her previous remark, "You know you want to," and boy did he, aware every minute of her doing yoga in the other room while he worked. On his way home, he remembered that Sharon was off today, so if Livy were out, maybe there could be a nooner.

He opened the back door calling out, "I'm home, babe," only to hear Livy yelling, "Don't tell her to loosen up, Tink."

Vince walked through the mudroom into the kitchen where a young man was sitting on their counter, arms wrapped around a camera as he argued with Livy. Another kid was fooling with a wire strung over the track lighting.

"But she's talking like it's a science experiment on public television."

"Dude, melting sugar is science." Livy turned her attention on Sharon next. "Now, explain your secret for not burning it. Do the sugar melt again. Here's another pan all measured." Vince stayed put near the door.

Sharon, face flushed and hair in a new style, restarted the process, looking into the cameras as she explained the mysteries of heating the sugar to a glistening amber syrup. She stopped once to backtrack, adding a tip about smoke.

Livy and the crew broke into the applause for the good take, then noticed Vince.

"Uncle Vince, meet Tink and Grant, film students. We're prepping Aunt Sharon and making videos. Isn't it cool they drove all the way here to help?"

Vince saw the quickie upstairs drop out of sight. *Had Livy already invited these guys for overnight or a week?* He glanced in the hall for telltale backpacks, but it was hard to say what with the camera equipment and, yes, his power cord and work light taking up space. He took Sharon aside.

"Is it helping?" he asked hopefully.

Much of their talk lately was devoted to her insecurities about the upcoming audition in Chicago. Maybe she should just drop the whole thing, but she wouldn't know unless she tried. *Right, Vince? Right, honey,* though he wondered what price success would exact from them. Would she make money, or would it cost them money? Would success take her beyond what he could offer in Elkhart? And his mother was hinting that she might name him the managing brother if Mike continued to show no flare for it. So there would go the time he tried to devote to Sharon's Desserts.

"Not at first. But this last time through, yes. We're going to end up with a lot of flan." She pointed to three empty egg cartons. "They haven't eaten yet. Can you make sandwiches? I'm too bushed, but I'll find drinks and plates."

Vince noticed their protests about not putting the D'Angelos to any trouble were pretty weak once he got out a hunk of pastrami, sauerkraut, cheese, mayo and a nonstick pan. Tink and Grant seemed to hang on his every move as he sliced off the meat, slathered the bread—*Gotta use rye*—and began to open the sauerkraut.

"Are you thinking what I'm thinking?" Grant said to Tink.

"Yeah, start rolling. This'll be perfect for the other part of the class project."

Though he hoped he wasn't upstaging Sharon, Vince couldn't resist an audience. Putting a dish towel at his waist, he went into overdrive with the sandwiches, adding a cautionary about mayo shortage or skimping on the butter spread on the outsides for grilling. "This isn't a ladies' tea sandwich," he said. He held the pan at an angle for a close-up of the pale cheese oozing out over the sauerkraut.

"That settles it, Vince. I'm sending you to the audition." Sharon gave him a kiss as she arranged the sandwiches on their plates.

"No, you're the chef, honey. Anyone can make a sandwich. Serving it is a whole 'nother thing. Witness this beautiful presentation, men."

Livy handed out the plates that did look like magazine pictures with the sandwiches snuggled next to chips, fresh pear slices, and homemade watermelon pickles. Sharon and Livy shared a sandwich and led everyone to take their plates out on the deck where the wind brought the scent of warming earth.

In spite of the lost noon hour quickie, Vince felt deep satisfaction in the scene, though short for him since he needed to get back to work. Here was their kitchen filled with young people of his wife's acquaintance rather than his family. *But would it last?* They couldn't go on forever ignoring that Livy's family might be a threat of some sort to their financial security, if not Sharon's deep attachments. And Betty, could she withstand this sort of revision of the sainted Charlie? And if the girl abandoned them, he hated to think of the loss for already he knew Sharon was thinking long range about how Livy could fit into their lives.

Vince took his plate to the sink. "Looks like there'll be plenty of flan later," he called to the deck. He was pleased Sharon followed him to his van. Perhaps some good news rather than worries would be delivered.

"Vincie?"—*a good sign*, he thought as he lingered to talk to his wife—"I'm going to send them to the shop about four o'clock to frost cupcakes. If you get home early, we can go upstairs." She kissed his cheek.

"Sure, it's a date." In the shelter of the van door he gave her a licentious squeeze.

21

A Time to Embrace?

Midway airport courtesy transport took the travelers
through what Ed called the bowels of the airport—
Betty would have said restricted areas—so they didn't have a
long walk to their gate. With a half-hour wait, they inspected their fellow passengers. Ed nudged her, whispering that
everyone getting on the plane looked "okay," while she was
analyzing people for their relationships. Most magnetic was
a mother with her daughter about Sharon's age. They chatted over photos on their phones. Just maybe, Betty thought,
she and Sharon could travel somewhere exciting, New York,
for instance, now that soon she would be an expert.

Ed was shifting around in his seat, Betty noticed. Not a
frequent flyer but a savvy one, she took charge. "The rest-
rooms are over there. You know how inconvenient the ones
are on the plane. I think I'll step over. You too?"

He followed her obediently, and she hoped his discom-
fort would be over. Soon their attention was on the lettered
lines for boarding, which went smoothly, and Ed led them
beyond the roomy seats where passengers were sipping

drinks and coffee. Betty edged along behind Ed, and he stopped to chat with the wearer of another USN cap before they found seats behind the wing. Betty noted Ed's manful hoist of their bags into the overhead bin.

"Lucky us! The safest place on the plane," he declared as they fitted themselves into adjacent seats.

Betty felt this location sacrificed a view, but she didn't say so. Then she realized that her daybook, which she had intended to update during the flight, was in her carry-on bove. Well, her observations about the limo and the flight would have to wait. *But suppose Ed wants to chat the whole flight?* She needed her daybook as defense.

"I'm sorry, Ed, but I need to get something from the outside pocket of my bag up there." Betty realized she had to scoot by Ed who had already pulled his seatbelt tight. The man in the aisle seat stood, however, and opened the compartment for her. Once more she slid by Ed, feeling the brim of the USN cap through her jacket, no telling where her derrière was. She opened the daybook with a purposeful air while the flight attendants prepared for takeoff.

Ed paid careful attention to the safety review, muttering "If the oxygen mask drops down, I'll drop dead" and "That young woman couldn't lift a sparrow" as the attendant waved index fingers toward the emergency doors. Then he felt under the seat for the life preserver.

"Yes, it's there," he reassured Betty.

"Maybe we'll fly over the lake. That would be a pretty view," she said hoping to stress the positive. She had paid little attention during the safety review. Really, what could any of them do in such a case? First class, protected from the rest of them by a chintzy curtain, would be the first to go nose down, according to Ed. Maybe there was justice in that.

The long taxi and lift-off were smooth, but as the landing gear retracted with a clunk Ed turned to her. "Are you a praying woman? Is that a Bible?" He clutched at her daybook.

Over the edge of the wing, Betty had been watching the remarkable way the ground raced beneath them, the houses shrinking, but the tone of his voice made her take his hand.

"I'm sure the Lord wants us to get to New York City just fine. The pilots know what they're doing. Take some deep breaths." She laced his willing fingers with hers, finding their warmth surprisingly appealing. He nodded and struggled through a few inhalations with her, the rise and fall of the coffee stain on his shirt confirming his compliance.

"Focus on the beauty of the earth and sky from here, Ed. Surely thankfulness for all this would be a helpful prayer." He took a few glances out the window, adjusted his cap, and nodded at her.

When the route did take them over Lake Michigan, Betty was thrilled to see the lake depth and weather revealed by color change. To keep Ed's thoughts from wandering to the life jacket, she entertained him with speculation about New York and gently rubbed his fingers. Then she thought of the popular verses from Ecclesiastes.

"This is our time to fly, Ed. We're not planting anymore, but in the time to uproot, maybe?"

He smiled at her. "I'm all right now. Look at those flight attendants. They do this for a living a few times a week."

"If you don't like to fly, why are we doing this?"

"Are you kidding? This is the biggest prize I've ever won. Besides, we won this together." He turned to her to sing, "'New York's, it's a helluva town.'"

Betty provided the next line softly to prevent his doing the whole chorus for her and the next row of passengers, and added, "At last I'll know why the 'Bronx is up and the Battery's down.'"

"I checked our itinerary," Ed said, opening a packet he pulled from his coat. "The company booked us on two tours. I think we'll be seeing all the big sights, the Battery included." He began to flip though maps and a travel book. Betty leaned in to listen to his recital of their itinerary, impressed with his mastery of the street and avenue grid.

The captain, who had looked about twenty to Ed and Betty, described the weather in New York and hoped the passengers were enjoying the flight. He added that there might be an occasional bump as they passed through upcoming clouds. With this news, Ed's grip on the tour book wrinkled the pages, but Betty felt no unease. As Solomon said, they moved through a cycle of life events. If this was her time to die, well, so be it. The sadness would be for those passengers whose full cycle would be cut short and for those who mourned them. The elderly passengers would be saved from Alzheimer's or heart failure—one could look at it that way. She pictured news of a crash making its way to Indiana, delivered with concern by news anchors in Chicago. Vince catching the report on the radio, Sharon rushing to find her mother's emailed flight numbers—Betty had complied with her itinerary request—Sharon weeping and turning to Mary D'Angelo for female solace, her head cradled on Mary's shelflike bosom. The little movie jarred to a halt. Betty berated herself for jealousy, and then looked at the bright side of the air disaster. Charlie's secret would go to the grave with her! Then reality struck. No, Eleanor would blab, for sure. *Your daughter deserves to know, Betty,* Eleanor had said only that morning while they waited for the limo.

Ed's head had rolled to rest on her shoulder, his panic leaving him with deep fatigue apparently, and he snored lightly, his lower lip moist. Not a pretty sight. Betty adjusted his weight and got out her pen and began to write. Ruminating again on the poetic verses in Ecclesiastes, Betty came to the lines about "a time to embrace and a time to refrain from embracing." Well, time would tell on that one. She checked her watch, about eleven hours to bedtime to be exact. She made a couple of lists for pros and cons.

LaGuardia airport felt like a foreign country as they made their way to the ground transportation area where they looked for a sign with their names. Sure enough, "Ed & Betty Conley" was printed in big letters. *Oh well. We'll see,* Betty thought as they rode in the black SUV along narrow lanes on worn parkways. The midwesterners were unimpressed with the state of New York until the skyline popped into view floating as lightly as a bathtub toy in the East River. Betty let out an "oh my" and wouldn't have been surprised if Ed said "gol-l-y." It was indeed the Big Apple, with the Empire State Building, a regal promise of a great city. Betty's spirits skyrocketed as they crossed the East River. She was on a lark in the greatest city in the world with well, not a great man, but a nice man, *a new man.* Her pink nightgown fluttered at the edge of her consciousness.

With aplomb, they handled registration at the grand Waldorf Astoria hotel—they were from Chicago after all. An awkward moment ensued when their room door closed them inside with an insinuating whoosh, but this was mediated by their discovery that the sales company had treated them to tickets, the higher priced skip-the-line ones, to the Empire State Building. They rushed out, catching a cab and parading somewhat guiltily past the unticketed.

Their excitement built as they faced security and the elevators, Ed mentioning King Kong every few minutes. Finally they stepped out onto the narrow deck on the 102nd floor. It was so romantic and patriotic to see the famous view. The river with the Statue of Liberty in the distance and the Chrysler Building up close just made Betty's heart sing. She knew Ed could feel it too. They saw other couples leaning close together for a photo, the thrill from the height drawing people close, even teenagers consenting to a quick hug from parents.

Ed covered Betty's hand with his and squeezed gently. A wave of emotion swept through Betty, more powerful than the thrill of the view. She recognized it as a profound sadness to see the city with a stranger—nice as he was—someone with whom she shared no past, no remember whens, no connection other than the recent weeks. A blessing in some ways, of course. Ed had no memories of her being angry or unreasonable. He didn't know about her difficult childhood or two miscarriages. He didn't know about Sharon's burst appendix and the subsequent anxiety. But since the past is part of what made her who she is now, this man would never truly know her. Thus the pleasure of the view was lessened because she knew this moment would not be a cherished memory another loved one could call up. How much she wished in that moment that Charlie were there with her. Or Sharon, someone she loved who would savor the moment with her now and who could keep its richness when she was gone.

"It's just so beautiful," said Betty. "I can't believe I'm really here."

"I know what you mean," Ed said. Betty turned toward him thinking he might say more, but he was staring into the distance his eyes glistening with a touch of patriotism or something else? Their hands remained clasped, warm and reassuring, but the feeling was without a spark. Ed patted her hand and let go.

They agreed it was way past time to look for some dinner. Back at their hotel, they studied menus for the hotel restaurants, but all were beyond their means.

"Too bad there's not a wills and trusts seminar going on," Ed said. "Could be New York lawyers don't have to drum up business like that."

Betty agreed that perhaps the Midwest was different with the free dinner thing. Next they set off on the street, pausing to look at posted menus until the sidewalk maître d's became too insistent. The international food offerings seemed too exotic for their first night. Betty felt her digestion was suffering from travel already.

"I just don't know what tagine is," Betty said looking at the menu at a Moroccan place. Ed wasn't sure either.

"Let's just go to McDonald's. We'll know what we're getting." Ed pointed across the street where even in the dazzle of Times Square the golden arches were unmistakable. They grumbled about the markup on the burgers, settled into a corner along the window to watch people pass by, and took sidelong glances at other customers. It was different from Chicago, though Betty wasn't sure she could say how.

Back at the hotel after another half hour strolling the lobbies, they headed upstairs tired out. They got the door open after several tries with the key card, the tiny alternating red and green light an icon of Betty's thoughts. Ed had placed their bags on the stands earlier following one of Eleanor's many cautions about New York—more bedbugs than Chicago.

Betty hung up her jacket and opened her suitcase. Should she get out her nightwear right away? It was already nine thirty. She glanced at Ed to see what his plan was. He was rustling a newspaper in front of the window, his profile against the city lights pleasingly upright and solid, perhaps accounting for her sense of safety on the street earlier with his hand at her elbow. She gathered her new gown and toothbrush. After all, Ed might be politely waiting for her to use the bathroom.

"I'll just duck in here," she said, her gown and robe draped over her arm, the toothbrush discretely in its case.

"Be my guest," Ed replied over the edge of the newspaper.

The dilemma of whether to take a shower was quickly answered in the white-tile-and-chrome bathroom by a full-length mirror. With the door closed against viewers, the room still promised no mercy for the naked. Even her accessories case looked woefully worn on the marble vanity. At least her cherry pink gown was new and modestly long. She delayed the shower and outfoxed the mirror by doing the final garment removal with her eyes closed. When she felt the length of satin fall into place, she took a look. *Well, there was a woman ready for action.* Eleanor had been right about a new gown. She felt pretty and desirable as the fabric swayed with her movements.

She stepped out into the bedroom. "It's all yours, Ed." She immediately regretted the remark with its unclear reference.

"Va-va-voom," he said looking at her as he hauled his suitcase into the bathroom. Betty gave a little twirl in response, though she felt Sharon's disapproval somewhere out there.

While Betty listened to the water splash in the shower, she paced the deep carpet in her slippers, being mindful of bedbugs. She regarded the beds held apart by a table with lamp, phone, and clock. The remote rested there too. Would Ed want to watch a movie? What kind? She realized how little she really knew about him. *And maybe that little was enough.* Let his predisposition for stroke or dementia stay hidden. He was okay now. Here was her chance to live a little, a modern widow.

After dimming the lights inside for a better view outside, she stood at the window. The city sounds crept into the room, different from Chicago somehow, more horns and wailing sirens echoing through air shafts in grimy buildings. She mused on Charlie and their first nights together on a honeymoon to Niagara Falls, of the novelty of first fulfillments of passion without restraint. She rocked slightly with her memories, her hand on the cool glass.

When a ghost appeared in the reflection, she yelped.

She whipped around using the nearby chair as a barrier against the white approaching column that reached for her.

"Betty?"

It was Ed in a full-length, white nightshirt.

She couldn't help herself—she fell not into his arms, which were outstretched to steady her, but into the chair, her giggles preventing any remarks, not that anything appropriate came to mind. Instead, images of breezes below threw her into hiccups.

"I'm sorry, Ed. I thought you were a ghost," she offered between gasps.

"The nightshirt? I just find it handy to get into. And they wear longer than pajamas. I see you have a nightgown on."

"Of course." She repressed analysis of his time-and-money-saving ideas and stood.

"I thought you were going to hit me with the chair." He picked it up. "It's pretty hefty."

"Now I need another scare to get rid of these hiccups." Betty tried holding her breath against another gasp, and Ed said "Boo!" politely and then brought her a glass of cold water. A final hiccup jarred her arm propelling water onto the pink gown and nightshirt.

"Sorry!" Betty pulled the gown away from her chest mindful of the clinging, wet fabric. "It was like a geyser."

"Did you say *geezer*?" Ed daubed her with a towel. "I could take offense."

"No, geyser, like—" But she couldn't finish. Ed had broken into a whooping "har-har" that made them both sit down.

"I've heard of throwing cold water on a fellow," he said.

She demurred over and over, and they laughed more until the beds could not be ignored any longer. New gown or not, Betty realized she did not want more romance. Maybe there was something wrong with her. It wasn't his unsophistication, or the nightshirt, or worrying what Sharon would think. It was just that the certain something was lacking.

"I'm just going to take the one near the bathroom, Ed." She flipped back the covers.

"Good. I'll be near the door in case of invaders."

She was surprised at the relief in his voice. Maybe she wasn't what he wanted either.

22

Sharon and Betty Pussyfoot Around

Betty had two versions of her New York trip, one for Eleanor and one for Sharon and Vince. The conversation with Sharon omitted any details about desire, or lack thereof, but was full of enthusiasm for travel. Each version chronicled the wonderful tours and eating at McDonald's and a small Sicilian place they discovered where the nice server asked about Chicago. They had felt quite like locals there as they toasted with Chianti over the checkered tablecloth. She really understood now why New York was the Big Apple, but it was hard to explain.

"I told Ed, 'It's a great place to visit, but I wouldn't want to live there,'" Betty said to Eleanor.

"You and lots of other people. But you haven't told me, what about you and Ed?"

"He's very nice." Though Betty believed in discretion, she explained her feelings to her friend. "I couldn't picture intimacy. I didn't want to know more, or show more, I guess you could say."

"What about his side? Was he asking for more?"

"Not really. The spark was lacking even for—"

"Making out to get in the mood?"

"I was going to say cuddling. Would that have done any good? Aren't we just too darn old for the spark?" The ladies fell silent.

With Betty in New York, Sharon had not worried about her popping in at the shop. Now that Betty was back in Illinois, Sharon knew she must keep tabs on her mother's every move to forestall any surprise visits. So on the phone Sharon encouraged her mother to exhaust all the details about the tours and dining.

Betty, happy to have her rapt attention, obliged with plenty of details, describing their search for a restaurant the first night.

"You ate at McDonald's, Mom? In New York City?"

Betty warmed to her daughter's interest. "We wanted to see how it was different from home. But we did go to other restaurants too the next day. Vince would have loved the Italian place. Oh, the desserts brought out on a tray were wonderful." Oops, she didn't want to imply they were superior to Sharon's. "Your fruited tarts would have fit right in."

"I'm definitely jealous. What a nice time. So, how was your man, Ed?"

Betty was surprised at the way Sharon referred to him.

"He's very nice. A gentleman." She hoped this said all that was needed.

"You may be seeing more of him now?"

"Maybe." In fact she wondered this herself. Would Ed call again now that their feelings for each other were clearly defined? "We'll probably have dinner or something."

Though that would depend on Ed's resources for freebies, which she kept unsaid. She had found out on the trip that he had slender means for retirement. Her own were more than adequate but not lavish either.

On her end, Sharon found the conversation with her mother a typically maddening one, where Betty detoured around the real landmark of interest while providing details about side roads. She interrupted her mother's description of a candy store in Times Square. "Mom, I'd like to know if you're interested in this guy or not. Do you and your lady friends call them boyfriends? Is he your boyfriend?"

"Well, we don't talk much about—" But Sharon persisted more than Betty expected.

"I heard your old bridge buddies talking about men and dating at the NuLook." That should get her mother's interest.

"What did they say?"

"That, that some men they heard about expect, well, want sex on the first date."

"Goodness. Who said that?" Betty couldn't imagine this coming up at senior center bridge.

Sharon smiled at how her mother took the bait. "The woman with the blue waves."

"That would be Ardyce. I wonder if she found this from experience." Betty's warmth conveyed her willingness to gossip.

"She was telling on someone else, I think."

"Naturally. Well, dear, to set your mind at rest, Ed is not a boyfriend."

"But, Mom, you're alone, you know, a widow."

Now, where was this going? Betty wondered. "Yes, I'm aware of that."

"I wouldn't mind if you had someone special, because actually recently—" This would be the place to introduce the subject of the Graveswells. Sharon wiped her clammy hand on her phone, readying to go on, but the pause let her mother get a word in.

"You'll be the first to know about him, Sharon Lynne."

Sharon knew her middle name meant the conversation was over, but her exasperation mounted. She wasn't a teenager. She should be able to talk with her mother about relationships. She pictured her mother reaching up her sleeve for a tissue and trying to hold the phone at the same time with her arthritic fingers. Was she alone at Eleanor's? Suppose this astonishing news about the Graveswells upset her into a spell or stroke? *Maybe the phone wasn't the place to introduce a step-sister and niece.* Sharon's intention wilted.

"Okay. I get it, Mom. You don't want to talk about it, but I'm all grown up now. We can talk about men."

"Other topics are much more interesting. Now, what about your cooking audition coming up?"

"If I practice much more on flan, we'll never want another one."

Sharon explained how acquaintances—of a friend— had done some video of her. She went on to describe that she had gotten instructions about the audition too. "I keep reminding myself that it's like the kitchen demos I used to give, Mom."

"And you were excellent with your peppy personality and skills. I'm sure you'll do fine in Chicago."

Forgetting all about being a grownup now, Sharon was buoyed by her mother's unshaken confidence in her. They parted with "love yous."

Sharon perused weather forecasts, tinkered with her shop website, and checked Facebook to repress her failure at revelation. A photo of Betty and Ed at the Empire State Building popped up, startling her. *Mother has a Facebook page?* She looked at the photo again. Ed seemed to have his arm around Betty. Not handsome, but healthy looking. That was probably enough at their age. Maybe the best policy would be to just keep the Graveswells a secret for a while. What was the harm in that?

Eleanor accosted Betty with her laptop when her conversation with Sharon ended.

"Betty, now that you're back from New York, you can plan to meet Juliette Graveswell. No more delays."

"You forget I did meet her."

"You know what I mean. Here's her studio address right here on her website. You can mail her a note to say you'll be in the Cultural Center on Thursday."

Eleanor handed her a notecard with a cougar on it.

"Do you have something less growly?" Betty laid the card aside.

Eleanor rummaged through her box of cards sent by groups she supported. "Elephants, pandas, or alligators?"

"Do you have just daisies or robins, even puppies?"

"They aren't endangered. Besides, the cougar is perfect with all the dating you've been doing lately. Didn't you say Ed was a year younger?"

"For heaven's sake, Eleanor." Betty was in no mood for repartee.

"Here. This notepaper is plain blue." Eleanor handed over a tablet and envelope. "I'm trying to help you lighten up. Now, I'll just leave you to your epistle."

Betty began to write: *Dear Ms. Graveswell: Your mother had an affair with my late husband.* She started over using *may have had*, but it seemed equally abrupt.

The blue tablet shrank. Any lines she thought of seemed wrong: *Dear Ms. Graveswell, Would you be interested in meeting your half-sister?* Or *Are you aware your father is not Mr. Graveswell but Mr. Miles, my late husband?* The lines she wanted to send were definitely wrong: *Are you a nice person or a conniving one? Did my husband, Charles Miles, love you too?*

Betty studied the cougar on the first notecard, which made her think of Irene Graveswell. "What's to say her daughter isn't just the same?" she said aloud.

After many false starts, Betty decided writing was not the way to approach this. She ripped up the all the pages, resolving to visit the artist Juliette again instead. Maybe it wasn't right to spring the information on her in person, but it cut suspenseful mail delays and left no paper trail.

Back in Elkhart, Vince came into their bedroom carrying a small wooden box.

"What's that?" Sharon took it from him and rattled it.

"I found it under a tarp in the van. Must have been from your mom's move to Shady Grove. It's photos."

Sharon took the box. "Oh yes. The box was in Dad's desk that we put in storage. I'll set it aside for Mom."

She took out the stack of photos, some black and whites, a few in color. The first few were reprints from her childhood that she had seen before in another album—one of her on horseback, another of her looking angelic as an acolyte at church, one taken on the porch swing with their cat, Blue Boy. In a photo of her in a scout uniform, she was laughing, probably because her dad was clowning around. He always claimed she looked too serious in photos, "like we're dull as-dust here."

Another batch was in color, their first Polaroids. How excited her dad had been about that Kodak Land camera. She had begged him for permission to take it to school, but he said it was for his work for insurance claims. Maybe these were claim photos since they were secured with a band. Half a dozen were of the same woman posed at a restaurant, on a couch, then holding a baby. In two more she was pushing a stroller, and in another she was holding the hand of the girl as a toddler. Sharon came to the last photo—the woman, the girl about four now, and Sharon herself!

"Vince! Did you look at these? This is me with these people."

"Do you remember the photo?" He turned it over looking for a date.

"I look about nine or ten." She moved it closer for a better look at her clothes.

"I'm wearing a church dress." Could this have been a trip to Chicago when her father had to go to agent meetings at the home office? They had even stayed in a fancy hotel, an unimaginable treat for the three of them.

"Vince, I do remember. Mother had a headache and Daddy took me with him to visit a client. That's what he called her. It must have been Mrs. Graveswell. Of all the nerve when mother was laid up." Sharon began to crumple the photo, but Vince took it from her.

"Wait, honey."

"Daddy wanted me to play dolls with that girl. I never played with baby dolls, and he knew that perfectly well. I was already mad at him for making us visit them when I could be back at the hotel swimming."

Sharon went on to describe how she had felt obligated to be polite anyway and read a story to the girl. "After we left I couldn't decide if Daddy was sad or happy, but he took me into a fancy gift store. He said I could pick out anything I wanted so I picked something big."

"Howie?" Vince named the fuzzy palomino pony that stood in a corner of their bedroom. Sharon nodded.

"He probably bought me Howie to keep me from talking about those people." *An early bribe for silence. A later one, my shop!* she thought.

"I always know when that horse is watching us." Vince offered his usual remark about their companion who, he could swear, occasionally gave him a manly wink.

"Well, he's seen it all." Sharon picked him up. "I don't know if I was ever taken to visit the Graveswells again. Probably not. Eventually I would have asked a million questions."

"You think that little girl in the photo with you is Livy's mother?"

"It must be." Sharon buried her nose in Howie's bristly neck where his straw stuffing poked through. His woolly scent hadn't worn off in all these years, taking her immediately to her yellow bedroom in their old house where family life had been simple. Her parents acted the way parents were supposed to. They hugged once in a while, kissed in private, and made her life easy and happy. Had this idyllic scene been as flimsy as a stage set, with her mother and her merely subplot, while rising action for her father took place elsewhere? Perhaps taking her to Chicago had been an effort at bringing the two stories together. And now it was left to her to pull off the denouement and even a curtain call.

"This photo would hurt Mother so much. She thought their marriage was perfect," Sharon said twisting her own wedding ring, a band of diamonds. "Maybe the past should just stay there where it won't hurt anyone."

They heard Livy come in and yell, "Hey? I'm home."

"You're ready to let this one go?" Vince gestured toward the voice downstairs.

"You and Howie both know the answer to that one." The pony's gaze was quizzical as Sharon shook his head in denial, his glass eyes bright. Howie had a few moth holes and a sparse tail but was still Howie. *Maybe it's a lesson,* she thought. Maybe there was a way they could all come out of this with just some straw sticking out. Maybe it was time to expose her father, but first she needed the whole story and it seemed the place to start was Juliette.

"I'm going to Chicago tomorrow, Vince, but don't tell Livy."

"Can't you wait until the weekend?"

Sharon explained how she'd read that Juliette would be at the Cultural Center the next afternoon. Vince disliked the trip to the city under most circumstances and didn't want her driving there alone. All the hazards from the nightly news seemed likely, slowdowns, truck rollovers, road rage, or a flat tire, but he couldn't take the day off. His wife had that look about her, so he could see she was going to go.

"Parking will cost you forty bucks. And then there's the tolls too. Take the train, if you have to go, babe."

They negotiated a plan where she would take the early interurban from South Bend since the schedule was more frequent than Amtrak's. They slept fitfully, her errand on both their minds.

Sharon got out of bed about three o'clock and went to her closet. *Good grief, this shouldn't be so hard,* she muttered. She had dressed for an event before but not for meeting a step-sister—a city woman and an artist. And Livy's mom on top of that. What would Livy choose from the closet? What kind of person would Livy want her aunt to be? Sharon shoved aside her black suit that Vince said looked like secondhand from early Hillary Clinton. He liked her sweaters with a hint of cleavage, but it wasn't date night. Livy had a way with color. Maybe there was something smart with color. She got out her best black pants, the ones that were the most trim. Black and white is always right, she recalled from somewhere, and found a black-and-white checked jacket that would serve since it was still chilly out. She'd had that jacket for a dog's age, but it had been expensive and her mother always said, "Money spent on a good label was money well spent." Actually, what she needed was her mother who had a whole new, very smart look. She hung the outfit on the closet doorknob, adding an orange scarf she hoped would be Livy's choice. Yes, it looked like what a nice but not clueless woman would wear. She would look like an aunt that could be trusted with Livy. She found a small handbag and heels. *There.* Now she could sleep.

23

Was It Karma?

*E*leanor insisted that she would come with Betty to the exhibit, especially since she had not sent the planned note to Juliette to introduce herself. They were going to have a late breakfast out before the time Juliette was supposed to arrive at her gallery.

"It'll be like a cold call," Betty told Eleanor. "That's when you call someone not expecting you or your business, according to my Charlie." She took a final look in the mirror and patted a little more concealer under her eyes. "I couldn't sleep thinking of what to wear."

"You look very nice, quite the city lady. Let's go." Eleanor held up a blue print jacket for her. "And see how I'm sacrificing my signature style by wearing beige on your behalf?"

"Yes, you're hardly noticeable in those goggles and purple hat." Betty nodded at Eleanor's oversized white sunglasses riding under the hat brim. Soon they stepped out of the building into bright sunshine.

Sharon's departure had occurred three hours earlier. Vince kept checking his watch as he ate a cinnamon bun he found on the counter. Sharon was supposed to call when she got to the city and then again after meeting Juliette. His phone rang.

"Okay, Vince, I'm here." Her voice was muffled by crowd sounds.

"What are you going to do now?"

"Scope out the bakeries and coffee shops for a while." They had made a list last night, shops she could cover in the Loop to get product ideas.

"So what time is that Juliette supposed to be there?" Vince wanted to set an alert on the nifty calendar Livy had shown him on this phone. Sharon reviewed the time, promising to call later.

"Love you, Vincie." The little dash of affection calmed his anxiety, until he saw Livy was standing in the doorway.

"Vincie?" Sharon was expecting reciprocity. He turned away from his niece.

"You too, yeah, you too." He slipped the phone in his pocket.

"Where's Aunt Sharon?"

He tried for an off-handed tone. "Chicago."

"To meet my mother, did you say? Why didn't she tell me?"

His niece's voice rose, signaling to Vince he'd better think fast. "She didn't want to put you in a difficult situation."

"I'd better be there too." Livy grabbed her phone and purse. "I'm going right now."

"There's no train until about noon and it leaves from South Bend." Maybe with insurmountable impediments, her resolve would weaken. He stated the case reasonably.

"Can you drive me to Chicago, please? Please, Uncle Vince." Livy consulted her phone for an estimated arrival time by car. "We can make it before one o'clock when my mom gets to her exhibition."

He peered at the phone app, and then explained that he had to meet other contractors at a job site. His mind raced ahead. Sharon had driven the sedan to South Bend, fortunately, he thought, since he couldn't imagine letting Livy drive alone to Chicago. He explained the car situation in detail, trying to sound regretful.

"What's going on?" Mary came in without knocking and caught the drift easily, though it was a new scene in this kitchen, a girl treating her son like a dad. Vince was trying to put his foot down.

"Please, can I take the van then? I'll be fine."

"It's too old for that trip. Besides…you just can't. Now, now, don't be mad at Aunt Sharon. She really wants to meet your mom, but alone in case of—well, I don't know what."

"But I want to be there!" A face-off had begun. Vince, unused to saying no, was trying reason to accommodate wife and niece.

"Vincenzo!" Mary raised her arms. "We'll use my car."

"Ma, you only drive to the mall."

"Don't be such a worrywart," she said, rolling her eyes and adding, "like your father."

Astonished at the only criticism he had ever heard her make about his father, he forgot to dither more about driving experience, the route, traffic, parking, and so forth.

"The girl can do the driving. It's settled. I'm going home to change." Surveying Livy's grey shirt over leggings, she went on, "You're going to drive my Cadillac, you put on something nice. Something girly."

As Vince heard the Caddy peel out of the drive, he got the picture. His mother had stumbled on a golden opportunity for dressing up, a city trip, and, above all, drama. He heard Livy's sandals slap up the stairs into their bedroom. Sharon's closet door squeaked. Ten minutes later when the tires spun into his drive again, Livy clattered downstairs in black heels and his wife's turquoise sweater over the leggings. A hot pink scarf made a headband and trailed down her shoulder.

Vince, knowing his role finally, reached for his wallet. He counted out six twenties, and said, "Here, treat Grandma right, I mean Mrs. D'Angelo."

After two horn blasts, Mary, in a jacket printed with sketches of European landmarks and worn over pink silk trousers, flung an oversized pink bag into the back seat and motioned for Livy to hurry up.

"That thing's probably a gas guzzler." Vince handed out two more twenties. "Call me!" he yelled as a kiss flew by him on Livy's way out the door.

At one o'clock, Betty and Eleanor, after too much coffee and a final ladies' room stop, walked toward the artist-in-residence exhibition in the Cultural Center. Breakfast conversation had centered on what Betty should say, until nerves finally got the better of her. "I'm just going to go with the spirit of the moment. Now, let's talk about something else."

Ten feet from the exhibition entrance, she faltered. How could she go through with this? "Maybe you should wait in the lobby, Eleanor."

"Of course not. Let's go in." Eleanor opened the glass door and guided Betty inside by the elbow.

The room was empty.

"For crying out loud, now what?" Eleanor said.

Betty felt relieved. *Maybe the Graveswell thing could just stay buried.* She was about to share her good pun with Eleanor when they heard the gallery door open.

About nine that morning, Sharon had felt quite revived upon arrival in Chicago, having slept for two hours on the train. Then popping into bakeries and buying samples had boosted her confidence in her own skills, as she had told Vince when she called. He had seemed a little *off* somehow as they said goodbye but was probably just distracted by work.

Sharon checked the time again. Yes, she could go find the exhibit room now. As she walked quickly north along Michigan Avenue, her heart thumped raggedly. She was about to meet her half-sister. Very soon, she would be like many other people. She too would have a sibling, and sisterly phrases played to the rhythm of her footsteps. *I called my sister... My sister says... My sister's coming for Thanksgiving...*

She reached the imposing Cultural Center on the corner of Washington and Michigan and paused by the bronze cow guarding the steps. Would her visit be like the proverbial bull—or cow—in a china shop? She saw that her upcoming revelation was oversized and unwieldy. At which point should she begin her story? With the unexpected inheritance of bonds, with Livy's arrival in Elkhart, with her silence to Betty, and perhaps most damning, her compliance with

Livy's lie about her whereabouts? So many delicate relationships might be broken by this revelation. She had ill-prepared herself with visions of sisterly hugs and happy tears. It might be more likely shouting, or worse, silence and weeping.

Sharon gently opened the glass door to the gallery with her head bent to delay the need to act. Once inside, she looked up to find her mother staring at her.

"Sharon Lynne! What on earth are you doing here? Why, you could knock me over with a feather. Eleanor, you remember my daughter."

Her mother's attitude seemed to verge on anxiety rather than the genuine pleasure of surprise. Sharon tried to hide her consternation at this hitch. When over a hundred miles divided them as of yesterday, why would they now be in the same place at the same time? *How could this possibly happen?*

"Mom, it's great fun to run into you." She improvised an excuse for being in the city unannounced. "I'm here for an afternoon of visiting bakeries."

"Eleanor and I are in the building for Scrabble, aren't we? Eleanor?"

Her mother's friend confirmed with only nods a recollection of their being introduced and the Scrabble date. Both older women appeared to wait with mouths open for further explanation about her presence.

"I came in the building to go to the restroom and this exhibit looked interesting." Sharon took a furtive look around and continued, "But I'm starving. Let's go to lunch." Getting her mother and Mrs. Goldman out was imperative because of her limited opportunity for meeting the artist alone. She would have to cut lunch short somehow.

"What a good idea." Betty put her purse on her shoulder. "Yes, I'm hungry too."

"We just ate breakfast," Eleanor said.

"Well, more coffee." Betty shoved her friend rather forcefully. Sharon noticed Mrs. Goldman seemed very reluctant to move along.

Behind them, the door opened and in came the artist, Juliette, in a whirl of a grey short skirt over calf-length leggings with a pale blue tunic. She wore black ballet flats and a slouch hat.

"I'm sorry I'm so late, ladies. Do look around. I'll be happy to answer any questions in a minute." She took off the hat, which freed her brown curls. Moving to put down her bag at a worktable brought her next to Sharon.

Betty saw a clear resemblance between Charlie and the two women. If only Sharon would not look at the art pieces, namely, the one with her father—their father—so clearly characterized. If only she could get Sharon out of the room, the sordid history could stay her secret, but Eleanor was getting in the way of this plan by making a meticulous examination of a sculpture.

Juliette and Sharon stood within a few feet of each other exchanging pleasantries, Juliette commenting on the nice weather, Sharon saying pointedly that she would return to the gallery after getting mother settled with coffee.

It sounds as if she has to water the horse, Betty thought. Though getting Sharon away was imperative, seeing the sisters together slowed her feet. She thought of Charlie, the good husband and provider who declared often that since he didn't like the city, why should he drag her along for a business meeting?

"Well, Chipper, here are the results of my staying home," Betty whispered fingering her anniversary necklace. How he must have longed for his daughters to be together but had resisted out of fear for his livelihood that depended on conventionality. Or out of love and deference to her and Sharon? She wasn't sure which.

Suddenly Betty felt that whatever forces at work had brought them together, to this same place—perhaps the affinity she and Sharon had always shared—clearly spoke to the necessity of truth telling. She should not be a part of her husband's duplicity. She owed her daughter that as her mother.

"Sharon, could we just please sit in the lobby?"

Sharon agreed with uncharacteristic speed to a plan she had not devised herself. They were only a couple of steps from the door when it flew open, knocking into Betty, who didn't take in the pink-haired girl, as she was too surprised to see Mary D'Angelo, of all people. Sharon's hand on her arm gave it a painful wrench then let go and gestured to Mary, who gave a wide-armed shrug.

"Mom!" The girl threw herself on Juliette. "Oh, Mom, you've met Aunt Sharon already?" She clapped her hands. "Aunt Sharon and Uncle Vince have been so nice to me. They are just the coolest."

"My God, Olivia. What did you do?" Juliette caught her daughter's shoulders and said, "You are so irresponsible." Then she turned to Sharon.

"I'm so sorry. I apologize for her behavior. Olivia gets an idea and then just acts without thinking things through. So impulsive with no regard for others, just like her father, my ex."

None of Sharon's practiced little speeches fit this scenario. And Betty was more startled by the Charlie-sounding reprimand than her realization that Juliette had a daughter Sharon already knew.

Animated by Livy's tears, Sharon offered all she could think of. "It's all right, really. Livy is very nice." She tried to pat Livy who was sandwiched between them. "We're glad to know her, uh, Juliette."

The women regarded each other in silence then offered scraps of sentences with neither taking the lead in explanation. Betty stepped back to find that Eleanor had put a chair behind her. *Of all the craziness of the year, this tops it all,* she thought and pulled hankies from her purse. At least she was prepared in one way for this debacle.

"Isn't this like one of those operas you want me to see?" Eleanor said in Betty's ear. "I hope there's not going to be swordplay or poison."

Betty nodded. The wronged wife and her daughter, the illegitimate daughter and her daughter! Only missing was the conniving mistress herself. Yes, it was an opera whose libretto might have more surprises.

"All we need is the painted paramour to appear stage right," Betty whispered. Eleanor smirked.

Sharon said finally, "You know, I think we've met before as kids." She described the visit she recalled, which Juliette confirmed. Yes, Sharon had refused to play with her dolls. The women laughed a little then looked away.

Sharon finally remembered Betty. She saw that her mother was sitting, holding her hankie, next to her city friend and Mary, a rapt audience. She knelt next to her mother's chair and took her hands.

"Mother, are you all right? This is such a shock for you."

"Of course I'm all right." Betty pulled back her fingers and tucked away the hankie, putting her hands in her jacket pockets. She wouldn't be soothed easily. "When were you planning on telling me you found out about your father's—"

"Dalliance?" put in Eleanor.

Mary huffed. "Such a fancy word for cheating."

Sharon glared at Mary. She coaxed her mother's hands from her pockets. "I asked you about the Graveswells after Livy came to our house, but it was too hard to explain. It seemed too hurtful. Daddy loved you so much. I know he did."

"And you too, dear." Betty put her palm on Sharon's cheek and went on, "But I discovered he had responsibility for her." She nodded toward Juliette. "I'll explain it all to you some other time. It's so unseemly." Then she took Sharon's hand and patted it.

Sharon knew it was her mother's way of dismissing a disagreeable subject. But it was not all right to treat this as if it were only a social gaff.

"You knew and you didn't tell me?" Sharon forgot about the audience in the room. "But no, you wouldn't have." Her tone was sarcastic.

She watched her mother rummage in her purse and offer a hankie like a white flag. Sharon held herself stiff. She wouldn't be so easily mollified, though she accepted the hankie out of need. They stared at each other.

Sharon wadded up the fine linen, which spoiled the crisp lace. Betty thought about the trouble she had gone to ironing it flat. This conversation wasn't over yet, obviously, Betty realized. More defending her decision was called for, even in front of these other people. She lowered her voice to speak in an aside to Sharon.

"I just found out about this last spring, dear. Remember emptying the safe deposit box in that fancy Chicago bank?"

"Of course. You gave me Daddy's surprise of the savings bonds that day."

"Well, believe me, I was pretty surprised to find bonds there for an Irene Graveswell, too." She stilled Sharon's fingers, which were twisting the hankie violently. "The woman told me, of course, that they were only friends, that he had helped her through a hard time in her life. But I wondered."

On the sidelines, Mary and Eleanor exchanged a glance and rolled their eyes.

"But you didn't want me to know, did you, Mother?"

Betty felt Sharon pull away. Oh, she could always be too impatient for explanations. "Your father was everything to you as a child so I—"

"Mother, I'm fifty-three years old now. You couldn't trust me with this discovery? Even *she* knew." Sharon pointed to Livy. "We could have made calls, or talked about it to share the shock. Now it's too late."

Betty felt that her disappointing show as a mother required more defense. "It's just so . . . so embarrassing. I wasn't enough for your father, I guess." She mopped her eyes cautiously with a pale green hankie whose tatted edge had starched hazardous points. Even in this situation, in extremis, Sharon noticed this useless perfection so typical of her mother's housekeeping.

"No," Mary said so loudly it echoed. "He wasn't enough of a man for you, Betty. I know all about *un marito*, a husband."

Hankie-less, Mary pressed each eye carefully with a finger to keep her mascara from running. "But ours are gone now, so let them rest in peace. We should go to lunch." She helped Betty straighten her jacket and scarf, murmuring many *there, theres.*

"Very sensible, Mary. My treat." Betty snapped her purse shut after collecting and stowing all the hankies. "How about if we leave the—the sisters here to get acquainted?"

Livy and her mother, who had lingered in the back corner, came toward the door, Juliette looking unsettled, Livy serene.

"Yes, let's let this pink girl show us some great shopping too." Mary pointed to Livy. "That sweater is better on her than you, Sharon, by the way. Just give it to her."

Though they had known each other fewer than twenty minutes, the sisters shared a glance at this assessment.

Eleanor added, "Very sensible suggestion. The young do wear things so well."

Juliette had more to say before the lunch party left. "Olivia, I really don't know where to begin with you." Though her volume was soft, her tone would have depressed the spirits of most daughters.

"It's turning out great just like I knew it would." Livy hugged herself then her mother. "Lighten up, Mom. Aunt Sharon and Uncle Vince weren't upset at all, right Aunt Sharon? So you shouldn't be either. And guess what? I'm going to change my major to foods tomorrow, or maybe later today, and I'm going to ask to intern at Sharon's Desserts. Someday I'll have my own—"

"Okay, Livy, take a breath," Juliette said as Mary marched Livy toward the door.

"This daughter drives you nuts sometimes, I see," Mary said not letting go of Livy. "Come on, Betty. Follow your half-granddaughter, or whatever she is. I have only boys. You're all so lucky."

Then Juliette turned the exhibition sign to *Closed*. Whether this defined the issues at hand, Sharon was unclear.

24

Chicken Pot Pie and More

*B*etty applauded Eleanor's suggestion of Macy's Walnut Room for lunch as they rode the escalators to the seventh floor, a perfect choice for Mary to get a big-city rush. Their table near the window had a grand view yet was quiet enough for conversation. Eleanor plied Livy with questions that allowed Betty to reconstruct the last couple of weeks. As she watched Livy, another legacy of her husband, she caught glimmers of a young Sharon, and her hand drifted to her anniversary necklace from Charlie, which she had taken to wearing every day, instead of saving it for—well, what?

As they waited to be served, Mary said, "You'll have to make up with your mother, Livy." Betty nodded, appreciating for once Mary's forthrightness.

"I was only following her advice when I searched out Aunt Sharon. 'Stick to something, Livy. Work at what you want.'" She mimicked Juliette quite well. "So, like, she can't stay mad very long." She shrugged and flipped her hair behind her ear.

Betty saw clearly in Livy Sharon as a teen, obstinate with an idea and somewhat unmindful of the results. Yet, Betty thought, Sharon's loyalty in trying to keep Charlie's infidelity from her was touching. How long would it be before her Sharon stopped accusing her of failing to treat her as an adult? Betty sighed, hardly aware of Mary and Livy's chatter.

Maybe what Sharon said was true—that she always had to have the upper hand as parent. But she was still a parent after all, something that didn't stop with a certain age, yet had she been the clueless one, building a relationship on superiority rather than equality with her daughter or even humility now in old age?

Busy with these tumbling thoughts, Betty said little and recognized her relief now that a decision about hiding or sharing the Graveswell secret was no longer necessary. And there was no doubt Charlie's granddaughter had made her way into Sharon's heart already, no matter the tarnish cast on her father. The expressions on Sharon's face had told her everything. This meant any personal reservations she herself might feel about this newcomer, or the girl's mother, must be set aside. Betty smiled vaguely and began to listen as Livy oozed excitement about the upcoming cooking audition.

The famous chicken pot pie was delicious, but Betty's fork slowed. Only two blocks away Charlie's two girls were getting acquainted. Goodness, Sharon would have a fit at this inept word choice—girls. They were Charlie's daughters, Sharon and Juliette. That word—daughters—would have to do, even if it stung a little. She set down her fork altogether. Oh, how she'd like to be a fly on the wall in the gallery right now.

"Betty?" Eleanor spoke again louder, "Earth to Betty! Are you all right?"

They all laughed, and then Betty said, "I was thinking about history."

Livy made a face.

"Not like a school subject, dear, but how the past isn't really gone and done with."

"Well, ladies," Eleanor said, "before Betty philosophizes us to sleep, we should finish up."

Betty smiled. She kept to herself her picture of history not as a straight narrative with dates on a timeline but as a narrative that meandered, not suited to erasure, but to arrows, carets with insertions, and an occasional strike-through. In fact, it looked much like her daybook, a messy affair—*well, there's a word to avoid*—a messy page that could lead to a good and complete story with alternate endings. She looked forward to getting back to her bedroom to make some notes about this between the blue covers.

Mary vetoed dessert in favor of Livy's suggestion that they go to a discount high-end retailer. Betty presented her credit card and helped Mary figure the tip.

"We do twenty percent in the city," she said breezily. Then they gathered their handbags and walked toward the elevators.

"Betty?" a man called out. "Betty Montgomery I'd know you anywhere." Their parade stopped and turned toward the voice. "Louie Nye. Elkhart, class of forty-nine. Go Tigers!" He stuck out his hand to Betty. "Remember me?"

A man with a snowy beard, curly like sheep's wool, stood in front of her. She studied his face, which had blue eyes buried in laugh lines. A few freckles showed above the beard.

"My goodness. My goodness." She took his hand. "Of course I do. Little Louie. You sat in front of me in Latin class. Whatever are you doing here?"

"Same as you. Lunch." Their hands stayed joined during the exclamation. "Say, did you have dessert yet? Coffee? I'd love to catch up."

"Catch up? It's been more than sixty years," Betty said.

"We'll start with the last twenty today. Do you all want coffee?" He looked at her friends.

"Oh, sorry. Where are my manners?" Betty extracted her hand to gesture. "This is my friend Eleanor Goldman from Chicago, and this is—"

"For heaven's sake, Betty." Eleanor quashed the introductions. "This isn't a reception line at a wake. We're charmed, I'm sure." She bobbed her head at the gentleman.

How could this self-possessed, bearded man with— yes—a gold earring be Louie Nye? Freckle Face, they had called him, Louie who couldn't fully conjugate a verb to save his soul or save himself from blushing purple. For the second time that day, Betty wondered whether it was coffee or a stiff drink she needed to settle the kaleidoscope of images from long ago.

"Or maybe we could meet another day?" Louie said. "I'm here all week for the Santa Claus convention. You can't believe how hard it is to park an Airstream in the city."

They nodded in sympathy with their attention now focused on his showpiece beard. "You're a Santa Claus?" Livy said. "That is so cool. They have a convention for that?"

"Of course, national ones. I'm even giving a workshop, on ho-ho-ho-ing."

"Seriously?"

"You bet, kiddo. Check my qualifications." He gave a rich laugh that turned shoppers' heads.

Mary got out a slip of paper and began to fidget with a pencil. "So, why don't you two exchange phone numbers. We're on our way shopping. Now."

Livy took charge. "Just put the numbers in your phones. Here let me."

"The young, so good with technology. Betty, give her your phone." Eleanor nudged sharply.

Finally the process was complete and the women made it onto a down elevator.

"So, you've met a granddaughter and run into an old flame," Eleanor said. "What else can happen today, huh?"

Betty offered no response. Indeed, it seemed nothing could surprise her now. She didn't even bother to correct Eleanor about the old flame.

25

The Art of Illusion

eft alone with Juliette, Sharon found that conversation was awkward, so she walked around to look at the exhibited pieces, odd as they were. She had seen Juliette's art online, but that wasn't the same as looking at it face-to-face. One sketch had beach chairs floating around in the trees, another had photos of women clipped from larger black and whites and reconstructed into other arrangements surrounded by rickrack. *If art represents the artist's worldview, then what does this stuff say about my half-sister?* Sharon pondered. This was not the kind of sibling she had imaged. Livy's characterization of her mother as "weird" she had dismissed as just teenage criticism.

Sharon couldn't help but notice that Juliette was younger and more striking, her name included. Where Sharon's hair was wavy, Juliette's had little curls. She had remarkable talent range from sculpture and collage to sketches, even if indecipherable. Sharon saw herself merely as cinnamon bun queen. What was her art but calorie ridden and yeasty next to these diaphanous dresses, sketches, and curious assemblages? And, of course, Juliette had a trump card, Olivia.

Thinking of Livy, Sharon wanted to soften the blow of her niece's defection from interior design to culinary arts, no matter how second rate to the visual. After all, the girl had first taken her aunt into her confidence —not her mother— about finding her passion. So Sharon painted a rosy picture describing Livy's proficiency in picking up the rhythms of the shop and inventing their very popular Mother's Day basket.

"Livy's creation entirely. I'm sure her talents come from you, Juliette." Her sister's smile encouraged her to go on about her niece's visit.

"Livy gets on great with my husband. She even talked him into getting a smartphone." Oh, this had not been the thing to say. It made Vince sound like a doofus in Indiana, indeed a country in-law.

"I'm glad they get along." Juliette's pleasure sounded faked to Sharon. Obviously she wasn't entirely pleased that Livy got on well with them and, really, Sharon could understand completely her reservation.

The women stopped in front of the picture of chairs hovering over the beach. With surprising honesty, Juliette described her difficulties as a single parent raising Olivia, who had always been immature and headstrong.

Juliette shook her head and said, "Olivia's father and I split up when she was six. I've had to be everything for her."

Perhaps the composition of chairs spoke of this insecurity, Sharon thought.

Juliette went on, "My sibs' father was hit by a train before I was born. As you may have heard."

Unsure whether to reveal how much Livy had told them, Sharon made a noncommittal nod. Juliette added, "So, I never had two parents at home either."

Did sisterhood require her to apologize for the good luck of two parents herself? Sharon offered, "Oh."

"It's not your fault, of course," Juliette said. "I don't think mother was expecting Mr. Miles to leave your mother." Her curls trembled. "Well, at least, not really in the end."

What? Sharon stopped in front of the collage of women, vintage 1950.

Of course her father would never have left them in Elkhart! Such a step on his part hadn't occurred to her at all. Why, they had a nice family house, her father was an Elk, she was a Girl Scout, and her mother cooked and sewed and cleaned and took care of them from A to Z, which her father appreciated a lot.

Didn't he?

"Was he at your house often?" Sharon turned away from the grinning women in the photos that were clipped into strips like dance lines. The rickrack framing was right for the '50s black and whites.

"Just a few times. I think mother saw him at the bank, mostly. They would go out for dinner or for—" Juliette shrugged. "I was just a kid, but I could see why Mom liked him."

Sharon turned back to the women who were all waiting for a man just like Charlie Miles, no doubt. Yes, her father was very likeable. In fact, he was popular everywhere, even with her childhood friends. *And obviously with married women who should have known better.* She wished she dared say that aloud.

"He could be a lot of fun," she said finally, but this seemed a confirmation of his propensity to fool around, so she added, "He was a very good father to me."

Juliette shared no corroborating memories, Sharon was glad to see, and she felt the tension lessen between them. They moved on to look at the little dresses that Betty had admired in her first visit.

"Like paper doll dresses," Sharon said. "These are really neat." Then she worried her compliment was lame.

"I like working with reality and illusion. The paper allows the layers to be transparent," Juliette explained about her process. "It looks like one layer but it's many. Like life, I think."

Sharon examined the pieces more closely. "Did you play with paper dolls? I had a lot of sets."

"So did I." Juliette laughed and pressed her palms together, a gesture Livy too used for delight. Then she touched Sharon gently.

The gesture gave Sharon the feeling she had anticipated hours before, warmth of a new kind. "Maybe we have other things in common too," she said.

"We'll have to see. Look, Livy was right to seek you out, but I just wish she had done it the right way."

Sharon could see her sister still had ambivalence. "Apparently no one else could find the right way either. Maybe there wasn't one. Look how my mother kept this a secret for over a year. You could say Livy broke the ice for us."

"She's good at that all right, and I'm glad you like her. She's my princess, though of course she thinks I'm just a pain." Juliette shook her head, adding, "Naturally, your mother may not care for either of us."

The conversation went no further because Livy, Eleanor, Betty, and Mary returned. Livy was saying that they had been too generous in shopping for her.

"Let us have the fun of overdoing it," Mary said with Betty agreeing. Juliette reached for her purse.

"No, no. It was on us." Mary and Betty brushed off Juliette's gesture.

The afternoon events had passed their apex, and the women got ready to part, knowing that feelings needed sorting out in private. Juliette agreed that Livy should return with Sharon and Mary because of her commitment to the Mother's Day basket project. Mary reminded Betty of the traditional Mother's Day dinner at her house. Betty protested that Mary went to too much trouble, and Mary assured her she would not hear of a Mother's Day celebrated at a restaurant.

"The family dinner will always be at my house. At home where the heart should be," Mary said.

Sharon wanted to point out her mother-in-law's mangled interpretation of the proverb, but she refrained. In present company, questions of where the heart is, or had been before, or should be were too delicate to discuss.

Mary, high on the role she had played in the day's events, insisted that Juliette and Livy also celebrate Mother's Day at her house. Betty was taken aback at this suggestion that could imply an invitation to Irene Graveswell. *This would be just too much.* Betty sniffed loudly much to Sharon's embarrassment.

"Mother is in Europe on a river cruise," Juliette said. "Thank you for the invitation, Mary. Suppose I drive your way Sunday, stop by a bit, and pick up Livy?" She paused. "If that's all right with everyone." She looked at Betty who nodded, adding that it would be lovely.

Unnoticed before, Juliette's city café sketch with Charlie clearly included seemed to leap off the wall to halt their departure.

"That's a real likeness to Daddy, uh, my father," Sharon moved in closer, blocking Betty's view.

"I did it from a photo Mother had. He had a nice body look, very man-about-town," Juliette said, forming with her slender hands a frame around him in the sketch.

"Quite so." Betty nodded.

"Very lifelike," said Mary.

"I wouldn't be surprised if he spoke," Eleanor said with enthusiasm.

"Would you like to have the sketch?" Juliette turned to Betty.

Would I? she pondered. Often in her widowhood she had made his photo a companion to fill moments of loneliness or indecision, even anger. This was a remarkable likeness in a city café where, with his newspaper, he looked completely at home among animated patrons. It filled her with regret because only now in her new life would she know how to fit into this urban picture too. Yet he had been there long before, making a life where he excluded them. Livy broke in between the two women.

"Wait, decide about the picture later. I have an idea for now. We need a wish circle."

"A witch circle?" Mary looked alarmed.

"Wish. Wish circle. We used to do it at camp. You write a wish on a piece of paper." Her companions looked puzzled.

"We write what we wish we could say to Mr. Miles, if he were here. It's a cleansing thing without the green juice."

"How fortunate." Eleanor made a face as Livy went on.

"Then you're supposed to throw the notes in a fire, but we can tear them into tiny pieces and throw them into the wind outside." She pressed her hands together with this inspiration and then tore into strips a page from the gallery guest book.

Juliette seemed unsurprised, as did Sharon, at this inventive suggestion. Betty said random words of protest, but Mary and Eleanor hustled her into cooperation, whispering they should humor the girl.

"You didn't even know him, so you're off the hook, Eleanor," said Betty as she found her pen. "Oh no. I have plenty to say." Eleanor wrote with gusto muttering, "just deserts."

"It's supposed to be like closure, not revenge." Livy looked meaningfully at Eleanor.

Five minutes later, Livy organized a trip to the walkway outside the building where a draft from the lake swept through.

"No sharing! Just shred and toss." Livy made a pirouette to demonstrate. The little pieces swirled away from their hands moments later.

Was this just new age foolishness? Betty wondered. But her heart felt lighter, and she couldn't help but think she could pry out of Sharon her message. Then she scolded herself for being the nosey mother. She hadn't changed a bit yet in spite of her resolutions.

26

An Evening of Decompression

In the evening, Betty and Eleanor were settled in the condo living room where they could decompress, as Eleanor put it. She brought in tea and raisin toast cut diagonally. A lazy Susan already on the coffee table held several small jars.

"Try some of the chocolate hazelnut stuff, Betty. I think you deserve it." Eleanor twirled the dish so the creamy spread landed in front of Betty. "I may just phone Maxine to come by and give you a massage, too."

"Oh, please no. For rejuvenation, I'll just spread extra chocolate on the toast."

"Maxine will bring her table and you could strip down to your—"

"I've only just adjusted to a pedi, Eleanor. Please."

"We can go tomorrow to the nail salon again, but don't say I didn't offer a massage tonight."

"I wouldn't think of faulting you. This goo is just the ticket." She bit into a heaped-up toast point.

Dispensing with the spreader, they plunged into the jar with spoons.

"So, how do you think it went?" Eleanor said.

"Actually," Betty began, her tongue coated with hazelnut butter, "it's just good to have it over with. I can see why Sharon is angry I didn't share, but Charlie's affair was my business after all."

"I agree, but Juliette and Livy are Sharon's business now."

"I just hope it's not too late in life for her to adjust to a sibling and all that that entails. I had sisters, you know."

"I can visualize there could be sparks between her and Juliette over Livy. Let's hope they remember the story of King Solomon and the disputed baby." Eleanor focused on scooping her spoon into some glossy marmalade.

Betty bristled. "Sharon isn't claiming Livy because she didn't have a child. I don't think the story fits at all."

The women began one of their arguments over interpretation, usually a gentle sparing after a movie or play.

"But you ignore the wisdom part!" Eleanor pressed on. "Solomon hoped one of the women would have the grace to claim that the other was the true mother rather than force him to use his sword to divide—"

"What a horrible image! All right, you win. Furthermore, I think that Sharon will have common sense without requiring an adjudicator with a threat."

"Or," Eleanor added, "that Juliette will have the grace to see that at this age Olivia needs a female adult confidant who is not a parent."

The women grew silent, thinking over the challenges of the future. Then Betty saw Eleanor's quirky smile that often preceded a probe.

"Has the truth set you free yet like your St. John text predicted?"

Betty took her time studying the tea leaves in her cup, as good a place as any to find the answer. The leaves fanned up in a V-shape rather like a bird in flight she was about to say, when her phone rang. She checked the screen.

"Goodness, it's Louie calling already."

Eleanor carried off the tea things, saying she would give her privacy, much to Betty's surprise.

"Hello?" Betty signaled thanks to her friend and settled on the couch.

About one o'clock, when Eleanor got up to take a pill, she looked in the living room to see Betty still curled up on the couch, her phone conversation muffled by the Persian afghan. Eleanor went to the kitchen, retrieved the charger, and tossed it on the couch, making several colorful gestures in passing.

Vince had spent the late afternoon straightening up the garage, an effort always appreciated by his wife. Then he tackled another task that might surprise her: wiping out the refrigerator after having a pre-dinner snack, or maybe it was dinner. Who knew what the status of their relationship would be on Sharon's return? Not alerting her to Mary and Livy's departure for Chicago might require considerable defense. Evidence of industriousness during her absence could help.

But before he could gauge the effect of the day's events, Sharon and Livy went to the shop to set dough for the next day's cinnamon rolls, so he was left with his mother's dramatic presentation of the Chicago encounter in which she played a central role, she assured him.

Finally, after Livy was safely ensconced in her earbuds in her bedroom, Sharon and Vince made it to their bedroom where Sharon threw herself on him in their bed.

"Whoa. I thought you were worn out," he said settling her beside him.

"Every time you called today, I felt so happy, even if I couldn't answer."

"Yeah, how come?" He fished for a compliment.

"Just because you were here at home waiting for me." It was hard to describe this feeling of her supreme wealth.

"You're not mad that I didn't warn you about Ma and Livy?"

"That was hours ago now, so no. Maybe it was for the best anyway."

"Get it all over with at once is what I figured."

"Except I'm still angry with Mother." Sharon sat up then flopped down again. "Suppose Livy had never come here on her own? I might not have ever known about the Graveswells."

"Your mom might have never found out either if your dad had emptied his safe deposit box." Vince resettled the pillows, but Sharon piled them up so she was almost sitting up again.

"I've thought about that too. Why did he let it go so long? Why not have the stuff sent here if he was too sick to go to Chicago? He just couldn't give up that woman is why. That makes me mad at him all over again." She tossed the extra pillow on the floor and their blanket slipped off.

"While you were gone today, Howie and I had a man-to-man talk about that." Vince brought the shabby horse with him when he got up to set the bedding right again.

"Now I find out what you do when I'm not here. So what did Howie think?" Sharon turned the animal so she could look in his glassy eyes.

"He said guys repress what they can't explain and then hope it'll all work out in the end."

"What insight!" She kissed the horse on his remaining ear.

"'Course you could say Howie's opinion is a just a horse's—"

"I get it! I think Howie's right." Straw poked her as she hugged the horse. "Daddy did want me to know about his affair because I'm sure he suspected about Juliette's paternity."

"He probably figured you would be the one to open the deposit box."

"In a million years he wouldn't think Mother would go on her own to a Chicago bank." They laughed, leaning back on the headboard until Vince tipped his head toward the stuffed toy.

"Babe, Howie just reminded me about how to make you forget to be mad at anyone."

"And how is that? Oh well, try me." Sharon put her chin on her husband's chest.

"Set Howie over there first. Facing the wall."

"Vincie!" Sharon got up and made a show of choosing the far corner, even draping her gown over the horse.

Vince watched her accentuate extra-fluid steps crossing the room. Then he made what he called his signature moves when she was settled in the sheets.

"M'mm. I've forgotten everything already, Mr. D'Angelo. So glad you were available on short notice."

"And you thought you were so tired." None of those TV rehabbers had it so good, he was sure.

27

Carpe Diem

Thank goodness Sharon had convinced her not to be stingy with minutes on her cell plan, not that they had been talking so much this week, what with Sharon's Mother's Day rush and the riff between them. Chats with Louie were eating the minutes like a hungry lion. They had the last sixty years to review after all, and there was much marveling at what youthful dreams had and had not come to fruition. She heard about how his military career had delayed marriage, and then about how the death of his wife had left him footloose for ten years. He described his summers working at national parks and playing Santa in the holiday season wherever he was, which right now was Elkhart since he was settling his sister's estate, which included the old family home.

Eleanor was hovering as Betty and Louie finished up what had been a short talk. True, Betty had been on the phone a lot when Eleanor was ready to play cards or watch a movie.

"Betty, you've probably used your whole month of minutes. The extra charge is highway robbery. Besides, isn't it about time you get together in person with this man?"

"I have plenty of minutes. And guess what, Louie and I are going out this evening."

"Tonight? That leaves way too little time for planning."

Was her friend's concern related to social considerations, or was she a little jealous of this man from the past? Betty wasn't sure.

"Louie's done the planning already. We're going to the Hancock building for light fare at the Signature Lounge on the ninety-sixth floor." Betty tried to tamp down her satisfaction at naming an impressive activity since Eleanor had hinted that Hoosiers lack sophistication.

"Oh my, that's pricey for a guy who lives in his Airstream. Where *do* you find these men?"

"I attract the eccentric for sure. There's definitely something wrong with me." Betty put both hands on her temples and studied her friend whose concern seemed genuine.

"Girl, we need to hit your closet. Look at the time." Eleanor brought her man-sized watch close to Betty's face.

"Just something simple will be fine. No need to dress to impress. Louie and I know each other very well already." *How many freckles did he have on the back of his neck?* She tried to recall, having counted them in Latin class. *Eighteen, no twenty-four,* if including the ones below the collar line.

"Some of your clothes are so old, he's already seen them. That blue sweater you've got on, for instance." Eleanor began harvesting fuzz balls from the sleeves that rode two inches above Betty's wrists.

"If only I still had my graduation dress," Betty said. "White dotted Swiss with lace collar and cuffs, perfect for the Hancock building. I was valedictorian of all thirty-five students in my class."

"I know you're one smart cookie, but you hold it under a bushel sometimes."

"But not so much anymore, do you think? And it's in great part thanks to you, my city chum." Betty gave Eleanor a hug and then gestured to her own bedside table with her blue daybook full of fliers about lectures, notes on web pages to check out, and blog entries for their project still in the planning stages. "Just look at my erudition now."

"I'll take any credit offered. Now for our closets." They rummaged and hung possibilities on doorknobs. When Eleanor asked her, "Which one says *smart and available* the best?" Betty felt she had misread her friend as jealous.

Within the hour, Betty, in a navy skirt, tangerine shell, and navy crocheted jacket, was handed like royalty into a taxi by Louie. They waved to Eleanor who stood outside in the warm evening.

"Ride the Tilt," she yelled as they pulled away.

Once at the ninety-sixth floor lounge, Betty saw that people stared at them on their way to the table. "You look like Santa on vacation," she whispered. But the attention was a lot of fun as she strolled grandly on Louie's arm.

Betty ordered sauvignon blanc in what sounded to her like perfect French.

Louie put his hand over hers. "Oh, spare me, dear! You're still showing me up just like Latin class."

"You ran circles around me in geometry though." Those horrible word problems involving acreage and yield had been too much like the farm she wanted to escape.

"I'll give you a geometry challenge right now. It'll be good for you. How tall is that building over there?" He handed her a pen and napkin reminding her to show her work. He went on, "If we know the Hancock is 1,000 feet, then estimate—" His freckles danced along the edge of his beard, a distraction as she jotted figures and sketched a drawing.

"An adequate job, Montgomery," he said after analyzing her efforts. His imitation of their imperious math teacher was perfect. Betty laughed. Louie was so entertaining, but he probably joked with many women, she reminded herself.

Timing the end of their meal with sunset, they arrived on the ninety-fourth floor at the 360 CHICAGO observation deck just in time. They took lots of photos, and Betty texted one to Sharon, who sent back, "Who are you with?"

Sharon had taken her up the Willis Tower twice in the past year on what Betty privately called guilt trips since she could tell Sharon believed that her inadequate provision of entertainment had caused the flight from assisted living. When a third trip had been proposed, Betty protested, "Please dear, your debt is paid," much to Sharon's surprise but not amusement. They had not done the Hancock building.

Transfixed, Betty kept Louie at the windows overlooking the lake well after the orange path on the water had turned to silver. Then the whole lake became an outlined void in the city lights where to the south the Ferris wheel on Navy Pier turned in majestic circles and traffic made Lake

Shore Drive a golden band. The Rhine maidens' treasure could not have been more desirable.

Betty felt for Louie's hand, which responded with a warm clasp, and she said, "That is one of the most beautiful sights I've ever seen."

It wasn't vast water like the Atlantic Ocean that she'd seen from Florida, of course, water that touched England and France, Brazil, Nigeria, thousands of places she expected never to go. Lake Michigan was her own big water nestled within states she knew. It was a lake terrifyingly grand in a storm yet comforting and familiar. She did not need to see these other places to feel thrilled.

"It says here this is one of the top ten views," Louie read from a sign.

"I'd say much better than off the Empire State Building." Betty had not thought of Ed all week, she realized.

They were looking at the displays and watching the traffic patterns below when a young woman took off a coat, revealing a wedding dress. Bystanders turned out to be guests who fell into place, creating an aisle for her. A quick wedding march played on a phone while a robed justice of the peace asked for their vows. The bride tossed her bouquet to a surprised young tourist. Soon security complained about this unauthorized event and the bottleneck it caused, but no arrests were made.

"We were young like that once," Betty said. "Think of all the days that couple has ahead." She considered how unimaginable the future would be to the bride and groom, even if projected in a slide show.

Later, still on the observation deck, now having coffee, they noticed that the café music had switched to big band music. Louie said, "Remember the sock hops after football games?"

"I spent a lot of time as a wallflower," Betty said, wondering if the boys ever noticed the line of girls by the water fountain.

"Now's my chance to get to dance with you. I was too bashful back then. Betty, may I have this foxtrot?" He stood.

"Here? I don't think—"

"Until security gets us, come on."

He led in a perfect box step. "It's just like the boys' gym after a game with Shorty Davidson on the sax. Listen to him swing." He hummed along, pulling her close so that she felt them become one dancer with the music. Louie maneuvered a whirl that made Betty lean back, her skirt twisting and releasing.

"This is so much fun. Just like that show on television." Betty stepped out and came in close again in fancy footwork that he followed.

"Do you think we'll get a ten?" Louie pulled them cheek-to-cheek, whispering, "Maybe the next one will be a tango."

"They wouldn't have allowed that in the boys' gym. Besides, I don't know how to tango." It could be rather naughty, she thought.

"Something for us to practice, then."

So he intended to see her again. Maybe this wasn't just a Chicago conference fling for him, like those Charlie had had apparently. How nice that she hadn't thought of Juliette and Livy for an hour, a record surely this week. They made a final fancy step, winning the applause of a couple at the bar just before a frown from security sent them back to their seats.

"You know what I was thinking, Louie, when the girl took off her coat and was a bride underneath?"

"That she was nuts?"

"No. What I've been feeling all night is that we're wearing cover-ups too. We can take these wrinkles, chicken waddles, or dark patches off at any time. And we'll be just like we were in high school, our real selves."

"You seem just the same to me now, Betty." He touched her face. "I feel like we've just had lunch. Hear the bell? It's time for Latin class. You've got your green pen, the one that leaks."

"You remember that?" It could be just a lucky guess. They all had fountain pens in those days, often leaky ones. She watched as Louie focused on empty space next to them and inhaled sharply.

"Miss Canalle just called on me to conjugate a verb," he whispered.

Betty offered him an invisible paper. "You better look at my homework. You're in trouble now." What would he think if he knew that during their class she had often counted the freckles on the back of his neck?

"Got it this time, Betty. *Amo, amas, amat,* and *amamus, amatis, amant.*" He picked up the pace as he got to the plural forms of we, you, they love turning it into a chant.

"Impressive!" she said, wondering what would possess anyone to refresh their memory of Latin conjugations. Maybe like her French course, it had been a lark. "You've been reviewing?"

"Yes, now that I have time and a reason. Do you need me to translate?"

"Why, no. You did the verb 'to love,' present tense." Actually, there had been twenty-four freckles, when his leaning forward brought to light the ones below his collar. *I wonder if they're still there?* Then realizing she had been staring, she offered, "I don't think I can match you with any French conjugations. I've only learned phrases like *Où sont les toilettes?* and *Je m'appelle Betty.*"

"I can't think of two more useful phrases at our age." His Santa Claus laugh drew attention as usual.

Betty felt his hand cover hers as he said, "Quiz me on another tense. Go ahead. Same verb." She felt him play with her fingers.

"How about the future tense?" she said. No point in making it too hard, like the perfect tenses that were for speculative actions or future action completed before a second action. The simple future tense was better in this game and one she might recall to offer a correction.

"*Amabo, ama—*" but he faltered on the second-person singular and caught her eye.

My goodness, I'd better be careful with this recall, she thought suddenly. It was only a game after all. She was pretending to draw a blank too when her phone buzzed with a text, which they agreed she should read since it was from Eleanor.

"*Ride the Tilt. I dare you.*" A winking emoticon followed. They read it twice.

"Eleanor has so many good ideas for other people." Betty put her phone away.

Louie ducked his head to look her in the eye. "I double dog dare you!"

Well!

Betty hiked her purse on her shoulder and strode toward the Hancock Center's thrill attraction, a glass platform window that tilted standing riders out over the city.

"I just might buy a ticket," she called over her shoulder. "And one for you too, Mister Double Dog Dare." Surely this would count toward her efforts at forgetting the Graveswell business for at least the rest of the evening.

From what they saw while waiting in line, the Tilt wasn't really a ride since there was no quick drop, just a tilt forward as if the window were giving way, a slo-mo play on a fear to induce an adrenaline rush.

Falling, Betty thought, the classic accident for the elderly. In fact, she had tossed out her favorite throw rug because Sharon made such a big fuss about it. *Falling for a scam,* another trap for the elderly, according to AARP. *Taking the fall* for someone could be noble but chancy, and *falling off the wagon*—there was risk everywhere you looked.

"Betty, it's our turn. Are you chickening out?"

"Certainly not. And don't you forget it's a double dog." Betty took her place between a set of upright railings. Louie stood in the next set.

As in a classic nightmare, there was plenty of time for thought as the window tilted at a crawl. *Falling!* World Trade Center victims had plunged to earth. She banished the image. But there was more. *Falling stars* and *falling in love,* and *fall,* her favorite season though a foreshadow of endings.

As the angle increased, Betty felt her feet's desire to slip forward. She tightened her grip on the rail with her left hand and moved her right to cover Louie's next to her as she said, "Guess what? I just remembered that future tense. *Amabo, amabis, amabit,* and *amabimus.*"

The window reached its full angle. Betty felt adrenaline from toes to temple.

"Really. *Amabimus!* Isn't that 'we will love'?" His freckles danced.

"Your translation is perfect this time," Betty said, adding to herself, *the spark at last.*

Louie gripped the rail and grappled with his phone. "Let's do a selfie. I need proof this isn't a battlefield conversion."

"Hurry, take it, Louie. I'm sure this is our best angle." They leaned toward each other as much as possible, trying for a kiss.

Eleanor and Sharon commented later that the photo arriving about midnight was certainly a surprise.

28

The Morning After

The midnight photo required much elucidation the next day. Eleanor pounded on Betty's door demanding she come to the kitchen, where over coffee and croissants, Eleanor held a debriefing. Though she meant to keep the most tender moments for her daybook, Betty described the early drinks and appetizers, the lovely sunset, and their foxtrot.

"I'm telling you, Eleanor, it was the strangest thing, like no time had passed since high school."

"So he made you forget about Charlie and so forth?"

"All that just didn't seem relevant." Indeed she had awoken early and written several pages, surprised at her new disinclination to fret over Sharon or rehash her marriage for clues of failings. "I just felt happy and..." She allowed a dramatic pause.

"What else? Go on, spill it." Eleanor's grip on her wrist made the phrase literal as coffee slopped.

"The spark. We both felt it!" She hadn't really meant to reveal this part, but it was a triumph, after all.

"Hallelujah, call AARP!" Eleanor grabbed the latest magazine, which had a sexy senior couple on the front, and pounded the breakfast table then begged for details.

"I can't explain it. It happened on the Tilt." Betty dropped her voice and went on, "I don't know, the fall forward or something just loosened or woke up, uh, things."

Eleanor's expression made sharing the detail completely worth it. "They should advertise it as an erotic experience," Eleanor declared.

"I just mean a realization fell into place for me. It was fun being with Ed, but getting acquainted was a lot of work in polite conversation, explanations, and so forth. And for what future?"

Even if she might feel more than warmth for these new men, she simply couldn't see herself in the role of caretaker or, for that matter, cared for after such short-term investment. *I'm probably a selfish person,* she had written more than once in her daybook.

"Louie and I already know how we started out. Now we have the fun of seeing how we turned out and maybe see what we can make of what's left, I guess."

"Kind of like a last chapter?"

"That sounds depressing."

"How about this?" Eleanor spoke slowly. "Charlie and your marriage to him were the significant plot elements and rising action. But not act five."

"I'm glad my life has provided you with theater as usual, Eleanor. But, yes, I think you're right. The Charlie years seemed like the end before. Now, maybe there's more." This was an optimistic analysis to match her good mood and they shared a hand squeeze.

Then they reviewed the upcoming busy week. They needed to prepare the bedroom for Sharon who would stay for the days required for the competition that began Tuesday after Mother's Day. Betty and Eleanor would go to Elkhart before the weekend to help Sharon and Livy because a newspaper feature had caused a rush for breakfast-in-bed baskets. As they finished their coffee, Betty's high spirits made her reiterate a plan she had urged on Eleanor before.

"You might find a new man yourself if you would go out."

"Goodness Betty, you're so liberated that now you're suggesting bigamy?"

Betty nearly dropped her cup. "I thought you were divorced!"

"Heavens no. Harry prefers his golf condo in Florida, and I like Chicago where there's much more action. We get together off and on such as for the cruise in August."

"Why didn't you tell me? Surely you would like to spend more time with your husband. I've been in the way here."

Betty felt her voice go shrill. She had had enough surprises about relationships this year. Now she discovered her friend—her best friend—had been duplicitous.

"See? You'd have worried and nagged. Our lifestyle suits Harry and me perfectly. And it keeps up the spark you were mooning about, without going on the Tilt."

Betty set down her cup hard enough to rattle the silverware. Apparently none of her people trusted her with sensitive information, Eleanor and Sharon, particularly. It was insufferable to have been misled by Eleanor. Had she made a fool of herself or been unkind thinking that Harry was an ex? Where did apologies need to begin?

"Betty?" Eleanor looked distressed. "I'm sorry for being secretive. I just thought our friendship would go better this way."

It was true. Her assumption that they were both single had built the friendship faster. Betty felt her irritation drain away. "Mrs. Harry Goldman, you never cease to amaze me." She began to pile the dishes.

"I plan to keep it that way, my chum." Eleanor rose with a dramatic sweep of her housecoat. "But with so many revelations flying around here, hadn't you better tell Sharon about Louie?" she said, pointing to Betty's phone.

The midnight photo had prompted a flurry of texts from Elkhart, one with an allusion to how she had mistrusted Sharon's ability to handle the news of her father's affair. It was time to talk, Betty agreed.

After apologizing for calling during the day, she went right to the subject of the photo. "I ran into a boy—well, man, of course—whom I knew in high school. In Macy's, of all places, at lunch."

"Seems to be the hot spot of senior romance, Mom."

Oh, it was good to hear the old Sharon Lynne with her funny remarks. Maybe telling her wouldn't be so difficult. "Louie and I, we've been on the phone a lot and got together last night. He's back in Elkhart for a while, so I'm wondering how you would feel about me seeing him—"

"From the photo, I'd say that ship has already sailed for you, Mom."

Betty took a quick look at the photo. Leaning together for a selfie kiss, they looked like big goldfish. She giggled then turned her attention back to Sharon who asked, "What about that Ed from the New York trip?"

"Oh, this is entirely different."

"I can see that from the photo. Where were you anyway?"

"The Tilt. I took a double dog dare after we foxtrotted in the café and…"

They settled into a long chat during which it was probably fortunate for Betty that Sharon was too occupied frosting cupcakes to offer any cautions or worries. The discussion concluded with a promise from Betty "to take it slow" and from Sharon to meet Louie soon.

29

Vince's Very Good Day

*M*other's Day dawn couldn't have been prettier, the D'Angelos and Livy commented while baking muffins and packing baskets. Only because the van held just three passengers were Betty and Eleanor prevented from helping or being underfoot at the shop. However, at seven Vince made a trip back to the house knowing they were likely to hike to the shop in their bathrobes rather than be left out of watching the baskets depart. Sharon agreed to this slight delay as long as they would agree to stay behind in the shop.

She considered how much of her good fortune she owed her husband these days as she made a final basket check. No one seemed more interested in her success than he did. He had helped out evenings and afternoons all week, given up his Saturday to clean out the van, surprised her with a magnetic sign for the door that read "Breakfast in Bed Arriving," and drove with her today.

Sharon studied his profile as he took them from one address to the next. Instead of being a burden, the extra work, Livy's disruption of the household routine, and the continuing demands from his mother had seemed to turn back the clock for him. Maybe they both dialed back a decade making their fifties only a rumor. For confirmation, she checked out her new look in the mirror.

Yesterday at noon, her mother had pressed five twenties into her hand. "Now you go right over to the NuLook, dear. Dolly is waiting to give you a hair treatment for when you're on television next week."

She had tried to give back the twenties. Betty seemed to be doing a lot of spending lately, something else to keep her eye on. "Mother, it's a competition in a studio. I won't be on television yet."

"My treat for the day is your hair." Her mother's new purse had shut with a magnetic snap.

Even my hairstyle isn't my decision, Sharon thought as Vince drove. She had agreed to go to the salon after her mother's promise that she and Eleanor "will just sit still" to mind the shop.

Of course they hadn't since they sold three more gift baskets after the deadline, and Eleanor set up the kitchen to make chocolate babka, a Jewish dessert that put together life's greatest pleasures she said, bread and chocolate. The complex project had kept them busy until evening, and with pretty good results, Sharon had to admit. Livy declared babka a selection for their ethnic treats.

"Wouldn't that be a good idea, Aunt Sharon? The new display case can be right over where..." Her three helpers babbled on about moving chairs and so forth.

And the hours at the salon had been worth it as collusion with Dolly had turned out a cut-and-color surprise. Sharon smiled in the van recalling family reactions.

From her niece: "Aunt Sharon, it's fabulous. So you."

From her mother: "Was that Dolly's idea?"

From her husband: "A mystery woman. I like it!"

The magenta highlights in her asymmetrical curly cut had been her own idea entirely she had informed them, not adding that Juliette's more stylish appearance had encouraged her to take this aesthetic leap.

The tunes Vince hummed told Sharon of his pleasure in the clockwork efficiency of the delivery route worked out by Livy with an app. She or Livy rang doorbells, handing baskets to excited kids or sleepy husbands. She reserved the high-end customers for herself, the Lauerbachs' in particular.

"Lila seems a little old for her kids to order breakfast in bed," Sharon said as they pulled up the long drive and Vince gave the lamp jockey a salute.

"The two of you have an acquaintance, I see."

"That was just for male bonding. Believe me, I was glad when this job was finished."

Sharon unloaded the rather large basket containing a floral piece as well as a half dozen mixed scones and muffins but only two napkins. A movement in the window confirmed someone was watching, but she was kept waiting on the porch until finally Lila opened the door only halfway and snatched the basket with no acknowledgment.

"I don't think Lila was expecting me," Sharon said when she got in the car.

"Somebody ordered a basket there."

"I think Lila was hoping for a delivery *man*." She emphasized the last word after noting that Livy was absorbed with her phone. "She came to the door herself. And only two napkins."

"In two napkins?"

"You wish." She poked Vince. "No, only two napkins in the basket."

"Maybe her husband is home."

"I hope so. It's sad when things go wrong like that." Sharon tipped her head on the seat and closed her eyes.

"I'm glad we're happy together, honey." He patted her knee. "Maybe you can take a nap before going over to Mom's at one."

Of course, their Mother's Day had really just begun. Vince's father, Manny, had insisted that mothers and nonnas be honored lavishly on this holiday. Even without him, the tradition must continue. Though the D'Angelo mothers toiled in their kitchens Saturday, on Sunday at Mary's they were served full plates, gifts, and little speeches by their children. Up to his death, Manny magnanimously organized a male kitchen cleanup brigade that resulted in his wife's staying up until midnight. Though all the D'Angelos were gracious to Betty and Sharon, and formerly her father, the Mileses didn't fill even a corner of the living room. Betty and Sharon always received pretty corsages from Vince, but as favorite uncle or cousin, he had many roles to play in the full house, often leaving them alone.

A companionable atmosphere filled the sedan in the ride over to Mary's. Vince whistled under his breath, with the buoyancy of a man driving four women in his car, all of whom were happy with him at the moment. He gave Sharon another celebratory squeeze for her triumph in the Mother's Day business. She was definitely arm candy in a shapely dress and in her new hairdo, partly thanks to Dolly, who was a sport in spite of his passing on her advances. He gave himself an attaboy. Since his mother knew all about the Graveswells, he feared no awkwardness there, and Betty, an even greater sport in his opinion, had thanked him for a corsage of yellow roses as well as for his kindness to Livy. And Eleanor, who seemed like a nice, if eccentric, friend for Betty, appeared to like him too. He was in the clear all the way around.

In the back seat, Betty smoothed her yellow print jacket and thought of past rides with Sharon and Vince. Lunching with them had been often the highlight of her month. *Well, things had changed, hadn't they?* She opened her purse and rummaged around to confirm she had her little photo album. Then she folded it open so that Charlie's picture was displayed. She patted him gently.

"Do you need a hankie?" Eleanor whispered and began to search her pockets.

"I'm fine, thank you." *Saying something makes it so.* She had read the phrase somewhere and repeated it softly now. This event could indeed be the test of the aphorism, so she added, "I think the party will be a hoot."

"Surely, you are mother of the year, Betty."

"Someone has to be," Betty said, shrugging then arranging her purse handle so that the bag would stay open. Livy, enclosed in earbuds, missed this forecast.

In the front seat, Sharon found her mind was a jumble—success of the basket deliveries colliding with delicacies of the upcoming introductions, though of course Mary would have primed everyone with the astonishing news of Charlie Miles's second family. And Livy would impress the D'Angelos since she was looking even more distinctive than usual in an ecru lace and linen dress.

Motion in the back seat made Sharon notice her mother fiddling with her purse. What did she have in that thing that she needed for a Mother's Day party? It looked as if she were airing a pet the way the bag hung open. Eleanor whispered something that made them snicker. Really, they carried on like teenagers, with Livy the sensible adult back there.

But her mother had been through a lot lately. If any of the D'Angelo clan said anything the least bit hurtful, she would walk out and take her mother with her. She flipped down the visor mirror to give her magenta curls a final scrunch. *Yes, they would walk right out.* Mary's Mother's Day shindig be damned.

Vince helped the ladies get out at the sidewalk and then saw a woman who must be Livy's mother walk toward the house too. He slowed down, unsure how to maintain the so far perfect day. Should he hoof it to smooth the way for his wife and her entourage, or dawdle and let her handle it? Too late for strategy. From the front door, his relatives spilled out onto the sidewalk like candy corn with his mother first out.

"Welcome to my home, everyone! Happy Mother's Day."

Sharon tried to get next to her mother, but Betty opened her arms like a diva toward the D'Angelos.

"My goodness, how nice that we could all get together. Let me introduce my guests." She turned toward her group. "Eleanor Goldman, my dear friend from Chicago, and this is Livy Riley, my late husband's granddaughter, a very dear member of our family, and her mother, Juliette Graveswell." To Sharon she went on, "Sharon Lynne, Vince, please help your niece get acquainted with the other young people."

Betty finished her speech with a crushing hug for Mary.

The gutsiness of this display quelled Sharon's irritation with her mother for referring to her by her full name as if she were in trouble. She glanced at Juliette for any sign of disdain, but her sister was warmly shaking hands with Vince. Juliette's other arm was around her daughter who was trying to pin a corsage on her mother's tied-dyed dress. Sharon rescued her sister from a jabbing, and the women sniffed the flowers.

"Look, you're wearing the almost same shade of blue." Livy pulled her mother and aunt together. "Mom, you always say color preference is genetic."

"So blue's your favorite too, Livy?" Vince grinned at her.

She made a face. "Actually, no."

"Another art theory down the drain." Juliette gave a thumbs-down that brought a full laugh all around.

Looking like a peony in a pink dress with a ruffled, plunging neckline, Mary led the group indoors for full introductions to other D'Angelos. Then she began a tour through her redecorated first floor in the modest house with zigzagging additions.

"Manny always wanted to build me a new place, but our sons were raised here. This is home," she said taking them to the living room.

Sharon dutifully joined the walk-through, admiring the new brocade three-piece sofa set and raw silk drapes that puddled on the oak floors. The center hallway displayed D'Angelos in many stages. Sharon stepped aside so Juliette would see their wedding photo, Vince in full tux and her, demure in long-sleeved lace. In the family room, Sharon was glad to see that the powdery landscapes by Vince's aunt had been hung this time at the proper height for good taste.

No point in Juliette thinking they were all clueless about art. Then she felt guilty for her snobbishness. The dining room had been repainted, but the furniture was unchanged, a nod to the years of family gatherings with Manny at the head of the table and Mary at the foot.

"I still expect to see Manny sitting there," Mary said with her hand at her throat before leading the way to the kitchen.

Sharon lingered to see whether nearly thirty years of visiting this dining room had softened the sting of the plaque at Mary's end of the table. *Una Mamma Italiana e Una Benedizione di Dio* in decorative script crowned a glazed floral motif, a reminder of a role she, as childless, had failed to ennoble, even with her second-rate Anglo heritage. It still hurt.

"That's an unusual plaque." Juliette too had remained.

"It was a wedding gift to Manny and Mary from Mary's mother. A subtle hint, you could say."

"It's beautiful angelica pottery. It's surely from Italy."

"Manny used to translate it for me on Mother's Day until it was obviously too late." Sharon saw sympathy in her sister's expression.

"I do some work in clay," Juliette said. "How about I make a plaque for your house. Something like *Una Mamma Betty e Una Benedizione di Dio*. Or maybe write it in English?"

"Mother will be taking Italian next, I imagine, so no translation needed." Sharon rolled her eyes. Juliette smiled.

"Seriously, Betty is so gracious to us, it's astonishing, considering."

"Mother believes people should get along. That's her whole life philosophy. Maybe that should go on the plaque too."

"I can make it as large as necessary." Juliette demonstrated a dimension that would take up half a wall, setting them laughing.

While Mary's other daughter-in-law and nieces were setting up the children's table, Betty settled on the patio where Sharon joined her. Betty turned sideways to hide what she had taken from her purse, but Sharon saw it.

"Dad's photo, Mom? Are you okay?"

Betty stood up with vigor. Her daughter always assumed she was on the brink of breakdown, so she answered brightly. "Oh, I was just giving your father an airing. It's kind of silly, really."

"What would Daddy think if he were here?"

Sharon's question was astute, one she had asked herself over and over. Today, she had a ready answer. "He would have been happy to see his daughters together."

"But what about his infidelity? How can we settle with that, Mom?"

"That's between him and me, dear." Betty put the photo away. "Now you go in and enjoy our guests."

Sharon saw that their extended family took up lots of space this year. In the kitchen, to an appreciative audience, Livy was predicting Sharon's success in the chef audition. Mary turned on the Food Network, and everyone leaned on counters while Livy did color commentary pointing out potential slipups and assuring them of Sharon's prowess. Juliette laughed along with the other women. Eleanor and Betty were quizzed for family recipes. Livy announced the soon-to-be-uploaded videos for Sharon's online channel. Only Vince's reminder of the dining room traditions prevented their eating right there standing up.

After many of the guests had gone home and Juliette and Livy had driven back to Chicago, the doorbell sent two youngsters racing to the front porch. They returned wide-eyed with the news "Santa Claus is here."

"It must be your man, Betty. Bring him in." As hostess, Mary quickly reorganized people on her new sofas so that the love seat was vacant. And she gave an order to Vince in the recliner. "Sit up, for heaven's sake."

As chaperoning daughter, Sharon stood to greet her mother's acquaintance. It did seem a bit odd that he was showing up on Mother's Day uninvited and rather late too, or had Mary, or Eleanor, or even her mother alerted him? They had all checked their phones within the last hour, she had observed. Of course she should have invited him formally to their house, but it was too late now for social graces.

Her mother sped into the hall from where they heard murmurs and laughter, and, as the couple entered, saw a mustache brush Betty's cheek.

"Is that her old school chum?" Vince said to Sharon.

"Yes, that's the guy in the photo." Sharon's immediate impression was positive. The man didn't look like a ne'er-do-well, as she had feared, and she felt guilty for thinking money was the reason someone might court her mother.

Betty fluttered with pleasure as she introduced Louie, and obediently the couple sat on the love seat. As a conversation starter, Eleanor described their serendipitous meeting in Macy's. While much talk followed to identify old Elkhart shared acquaintances and haunts, Sharon just listened. Her mother seemed happily transported to an earlier time, one that precluded herself and her father, which did rankle a little.

An hour later, Louie took a small box from his pocket and handed it to Betty. "Something for you."

Betty saw his cheeks twitch, which set the freckles dancing. She held the box midair, feeling much on display.

"Hurry up. Open it. He's not getting any younger." Eleanor offered her favorite reminder, which the family and Louie affirmed.

Betty slid off the ribbon, sending up a silent prayer. *Please be a pin or even a pill case.*

Sharon found she was holding her breath, and Vince sent the old guy a silent attaboy.

Betty removed the lid. There nestled in the cotton was a key on a fob with an enameled bird. People leaned in to see better.

"Your own key to the Airstream, my dear!"

The room erupted in applause.

Eleanor cried, "Your starship *Enterprise!*"

Betty giggled. "My goodness, my goodness, Louie." His Santa Claus laugh set the room applauding again.

After such a finale, the Mother's Day revelers went home. Betty left with Louie so that she could see the Airstream, which was parked at his family home on the other side of town.

"Don't wait up," Mary said to Sharon as she walked with her, Eleanor, and Vince to their car.

Upstairs in their bedroom, Sharon said, "Should I leave the door open for Mother?" It was nearly eleven.

"Maybe Louie invited her to see his etchings, honey."

"Vince!" Sharon made a face. "I can't even think about Mother like that. Besides—"

"Besides what? They're too old? We'd better get started on our next thirty years, then. Time's a-wasting, babe."

They fell into bed with Sharon reminding him that Eleanor was in the next room and that she and Eleanor had to catch Amtrak early the next morning. About midnight, Sharon heard the front door and went downstairs.

"Mom?"

"I was hoping you would still be up." Betty headed toward the kitchen.

"I was concerned about—"

"He didn't want to show me his etchings, dear."

"Mom!"

"At least not yet." Betty paused then laughed. "I wish you could see your face, Sharon Lynne."

"Well—" Sharon turned away to set out milk to warm up.

"Remember when Livy had us make a wish circle?" Betty sat down at the kitchen table when the milk was ready. "I want you to know what I wished that I could say to your father."

"I think it's supposed stay a secret."

"No, you need to hear. Your father loved us. I'm sure of that, but he had longings for a different, larger life than small town insurance."

"So you're excusing him on the basis of career frustration?" This was so typical of her mother's generation, a man's fulfillment being primary.

"Not when you put it that way. I simply mean that we can't know all he was feeling, and also, people make mistakes they can't undo."

Trite but true, of course, Sharon thought. "Okay," she said, glancing at the clock to confirm the late hour.

"For the wish circle, dear, my paper said, 'I'm moving on.'"

An acid condemnation wouldn't have been like her mother at all, but this sentiment was a surprise to Sharon. She expected that forgiveness would have been her mother's theme.

Betty finished her milk and regarded her daughter, who was, in her eyes, always pretty no matter in what disarray. It was time to offer motherly assurance. "I want you to feel free to be close with your niece and sister, if it works out that way." She took Sharon's hand.

"That goes for you too with Louie, Mom. He seems like a very nice man."

They sat for a few minutes more in the dim kitchen.

30

Starships

Sharon was right that their night would be short, but there was little to do in the dawn. Vince carried out her suitcase, which was packed with two new outfits she thought suitable for the audition. Though unsure she would be permitted to use it, she tucked in her favorite flan cookware too. Eleanor came downstairs at the right moment for departure as rail companion and city hostess. The trio tiptoed out so as not to wake Betty, though she would probably be cross at missing a chance to say good luck one more time.

Only a handful of people waited for the Lake Shore Limited. When the whistle sounded at a crossing a few blocks away, the squeal of tires much closer made Vince whirl around. His mother's Cadillac stopped across two blue-marked parking spaces, and the driver's door opened so vigorously that it nearly bounced shut on Mary's leg. The passenger door opened more gently and Betty got out.

"They never give up!" Sharon said looking to Vince for help. Did they think they were going to Chicago too? With so much human baggage, she could never concentrate on the audition.

When Mary popped the trunk, a whirl of silver balloons erupted, but Betty grabbed the strings in time, handing some to Vince. Then Mary rummaged in the trunk, getting something that required the three of them to duck down, followed by Mary appearing with a tray loaded with cookies.

"Happy trails from Sharon's Desserts!" she singsonged, thrusting the tray toward the little group of passengers. Betty handed out napkins. Sharon saw the surprise was clearly a triumph of their own.

"I forgot to serve your Mother's Day cookies, so we just thought that..." Mary went on, describing a midnight visit to the big box store for balloons while Betty was with Louie. This morning Betty had hidden in the pantry until Mary picked her up. Both reminded Vince to get many photos for Livy.

As Sharon followed Eleanor up the steps to board, she heard Vince call for her to turn around for another photo. Her mother, Mary, and even Vince had put on flowered aprons pilfered from the store.

"Don't worry about a thing while you're away, honey," Vince called out. "We've got it covered." He drew Betty and Mary into a conga line shuffle.

Sharon settled into her seat next to Eleanor. She had a feeling that she was going to ace the audition. And there ready in posy aprons was the answer to who would run the business if she were good enough to get a weekly show. And Livy was coming back to do an internship for the summer.

The train pulled away.

Betty kept waving wildly, so proud and happy she was about to burst. She was sure Sharon would finish in first place—*mothers know these things*—but even if Sharon didn't, she would be busy with mentoring her niece. Betty could picture no greater pleasure for her daughter and Vince.

Betty watched the train until it disappeared. Had it been only a year since she herself had caught the Lake Shore Limited for Chicago, been arrested, and as a result met Eleanor? It seemed half a lifetime ago. A few tears were coming. Reaching for her hankie, she felt the key ring she had put in her pocket. What was it Eleanor and Louie called the Airstream? A starship *Enterprise*.

Yes, she was moving on.

Acknowledgements

My thanks to many readers of my debut novel *Escape from Assisted Living* who asked, "What's happening now with Betty, Sharon, and Vince?" I've been happy to spend three more years with the Miles-D'Angelo families to write *One More Foxtrot*. My writing groups and the Indiana Consortium of Writers were very helpful listeners and critics. Thank you so much, Stephanie Medlock, Rosamond Potter, Elizabeth Frenzel, and Marie Greenhagen for listening over lunches to my ruminations on plot and then reading the final draft. Editor Kelley Finefrock-Creed worked magic on style and correctness and I thank her a lot.

Also, I'd like to remark on the valuable writing program for seniors, GeNarrations, a collaboration between the Goodman Theater and the City of Chicago. The friends I've made there as we share first person narratives provide substance in many ways for my stories. Their rich lives as seniors are an inspiration. Particular recognition should go to Julie Ganey for her excellent teaching and leadership, as well as for providing performance opportunities for us.

My husband and our daughter and her family who all offered frequent encouragement deserve my thanks too.

Joyce Burd Hicks lives in northwest Indiana with her husband and pets. Visit joycebhicks.com for links to her published stories. *One More Foxtrot* is her second novel about an Indiana family introduced in *Escape from Assisted Living*.

Escape from Assisted Living

From the landmarks of Chicago to the wrong side of the law, Betty Miles' escape from senior living and her daughter's quest to bring her home tests everyone's assumptions about old age, family, and the kindness of secrets. Sharon D'Angelo thought it was a solid plan to move her widowed mother into a senior care facility. But after just three weeks, the octogenarian leaves via Amtrak when she learns there's a safe deposit box stashed away filled with who-knows-what. She has to find the truth, no matter the consequences.

Sharon is devastated to find Betty gone; a good daughter wouldn't lose her mother like this. She and her husband Vince trail after Betty, discovering along the way that their struggling marriage has its own secrets to confront and that a journey can change a family just as much as it can change an individual. (First in the Betty books.)

Unexpected Guests at Blackbird Lodge

Charlotte often agonizes over her unfinished novel, picturing a different life than innkeeper with her husband Will. Too late she's informed a man from her past, a sexy noted author, will star in a writers' workshop she booked to shore up the lodge finances. Their reunion and a secret Charlotte might be compelled to reveal will spark domestic fireworks or the fulfillment of old dreams.

How could a week get any more complicated?

More surprises—another ex's arrival, an unsolved murder revived, coded guestbook messages, and daughter Alice's woke requests. Charlotte has her hands full, all while hiding an emotional roller-coaster ride as the lodge oozes with creative and erotic vibes.

Will Charlotte be able to salvage her marriage by the time the week is over? *Will she want to?*

Made in the USA
Las Vegas, NV
30 November 2023